NOVICE MYSTERY

MEXICO

The Second Dan and Karen Novice Mystery

Donna Rewolinski

Ten|16
PRESS

www.ten16press.com - Waukesha, WI

Novice Mystery - Mexico: The Second Dan and Karen Novice Mystery
Copyrighted © 2020 Donna Rewolinski
ISBN 978-1-64538-202-7
First Edition

Novice Mystery - Mexico: The Second Dan and Karen Novice Mystery
by Donna Rewolinski

For information, please contact:

www.ten16press.com
Waukesha, WI

Cover design by James Hass

First, I'd like to thank James Hass for his willingness to share his artistic gift in designing this book cover. James wasn't satisfied until I said, "I love it." James, I LOVE it.

I wish to again thank my husband, Frank, for all of his love, support, and encouragement, as well as his technical contributions. Also, I want to thank Holly Schoenecker, Kim Suhr, Lauren Blue, and the members of the Thursday night Red Oak Writer's critique group, who have read through my edits and rewrites. I appreciate all of your feedback.

CHAPTER 1

My back pressed against the plane seat, I survey debarking passengers. I'm vaguely aware that someone is talking.

"... ruins of the pyramids of Tenochtitlán, and I'm sure you're not gonna miss the Jose Cuervo Express."

Garbled Spanish words over the PA system give us instructions on connecting flights and other information.

I realize that Karen, my wife, is talking to me, but I haven't been fully listening. "What? We have to catch a train now that we've landed in Mexico? Is that what you said?"

"Daniel Novice! You're not listening to me."

I reply, "Karen, you're right, but the guy sitting three rows ahead of us on the left makes me nervous. He's bothered me since we boarded."

He looks like a guy on a 'Most Wanted' poster I saw.

Karen's jaw twitches, and a sly smile crosses her face. "Stop with the threat assessment. Armando asked us down for a visit. *Vacation.*" Her eyes dance with amusement. "This time you *will* vacation and like it. Please, not another Ireland. Any more police work on vacation and *you* may be a victim. *Of my wrath.*"

"Oh," I say as Karen jabs an elbow into my ribs.

She's right. The last vacation we took was to the village of Ballyram, Ireland, where I ended up helping solve two murders. Or rather, Karen did. "You're right, I owe you! This time, no police work." A smirk flickers at the edge of my mouth. "I'm just happy for Army that he got his dream of being Chief of Police in his hometown."

Karen crosses her arms and looks directly at me. "Just because he's the chief here doesn't mean you have to be co-chief, assistant chief, or friend-and-partner-chief. Am I making myself *clear*?"

"Yes, sir. Madam. Love of my life."

Karen snorts a laugh in reply. We're the last off the plane. No hurry since we are on vacation.

We find our suitcases, drag them to customs, and get in line. This department follows the same 'institutional-blah' decorating style of every such area the world over. Square rooms, grey walls, nondescript speckled flooring, chained-in lanes, bad lighting, and air that smells of plastic seats, stale sweat, and cinnamon—or maybe limes. Or something. Karen and I snail our way through the line with nothing to do but people-watch. The woman ahead of me wearing support hose and sequined sandals stumbles over her wheeled carry-on, again. The room buzzes with the low hum of a mixture of Spanish, English, and my favorite, "Spanglish." Finally, we're directed to the next agent, "Passports." No chit-chat, all business. Karen smiles and hands her passport to the agent. I join her. Except I don't smile.

Passports stamped and vacation ahead of us, Karen says, "Glad that's done. What did you do to annoy that customs agent?"

"I don't know. I've been questioned on the witness stand by a pit-bull defense attorney that was easier than that guy. Maybe he could smell cop on me."

"*Former* cop. Let's just find Armando."

Tugging luggage behind us, we make our way toward the airport exit. We step into the reception area where families and friends greet arrivals. I see a face in the crowd that has been my friend, partner, and confidant for over twenty-five years. Armando Gómez hasn't changed much since we first worked together, except his hair apparently stayed in Watson because he's nearly bald. He's built slightly smaller than I am, with square shoulders and a permanent tan. Next to him, I look like a giant glass of milk.

"¡Buenas tardes, amigos! Welcome to México. It has been too many years since I have seen you both," Armando says with a big smile.

We exchange handshakes and hugs, and Army insists on carrying Karen's suitcase to his car. When we step out of the airport, the late afternoon sunlight and lush colors take my breath away.

Army turns to me. "What is wrong, my friend? Did you forget something inside?"

"No. Your country is in Technicolor, even during the winter. Bright sun, blue skies, green trees, and flowers of every color in bloom!" I state. "Watson is currently fifty shades of grey, and not in a fun way. Choices range from low-hanging grey clouds, ice, snow, sleet, general gloom, and let's not forget COLD!"

"I have not forgotten. I do not miss that part of living 'up north,' as you would say. Please, let us get to the car. My wife will surely have dinner waiting for us." Army motions for us to start moving.

On our way to the car, Army tells us it will take about two hours to get to his hometown, Curva del Río Sur. He says it slowly for us to repeat.

"That means 'South River Bend,' right?" I inquire.

"Sí, I may have you speaking Spanish fluently before you leave. It is a great town. Peaceful and friendly." We reach the Chevy Trailblazer, load our luggage, get in, and pull out of the parking structure. "Eva and I are excited that you will be staying with us. I have missed you, my friend."

Karen pipes up from the back seat, "How big is your town?"

Army states. "We have about 2,000 people, and with tourists, more. What we lack in humans we make up for in cattle and horses."

"That's right, your father was a cattle rancher before he died," I comment.

"Sí, my brothers and I grew up riding horses and driving cattle to various pastures and to market."

"I remember you talking about it."

"And after college in the U.S., I found a good job with you."

"I know you always dreamed of coming back here and being the chief."

"Now I am," Army says with a smile.

"I am happy for you, my friend, and for Eva. What's crime like down here?" I ask.

Karen scoffs from the back seat.

"Cattle rustling is still a big problem. The money is good. Thieves are better equipped and organized nowadays.

My head pops up, and I sit up straight, grinning. Karen reads my mind. "No! This isn't a '60s television Western. You are not playing Marshal Dillon."

"I'm not Marshal Dillon, he is." I point to Army. "I'd be Festus, the deputy."

Sarcastically, Karen replies, "You'd be single."

"I think Festus was single." I can't let an opportunity like that pass. Karen stares at me, not smiling. Laughing, I let that subject drop for now.

As we continue to drive towards Army's hometown, the rosy sunset fades into twilight. Soft hues of orange and amber emerge on the horizon. Lights from houses come on and drift into the background as the road leads us into a more rural area. It's nearly dark outside when we arrive in town. Row houses line a street only a car and a half wide, and Army's place is a one-story row house at the end of the block. He parks on the driveway at the back of the house, where I see a garage and three-stall stable. As I step out of the truck, the smells of gasoline, hay, and horse manure reach my nose. Karen is first through the kitchen door, and Army and I follow carrying the luggage.

"¡Hola! ¿Cómo estás?" I meet Eva's dark brown eyes and broad smile. Soft red highlights throughout her deep brown hair dance in the light as she hugs Karen. The smell of cilantro and taco seasoning remind my stomach that I haven't eaten in hours. The warmth of the room wraps around me.

"Muy bien, gracias, amiga. I have missed you," Karen replies.

Eva turns her attention to me and gives me a hug. "Please, sit. I'm sure you both are starving by now." She gestures to a Formica-topped stainless-steel table and four chairs set for dinner.

Rich brown cabinets line one wall while the opposite side is open to the living room. The well-worn table sits in the middle of the kitchen, and a small refrigerator and avocado-green stove occupy the far wall. As if reading my mind, Eva states, "Army, put the bags in Dan and Karen's room while I pull dinner from the oven. Army's sister, Sara, is the best Mexican cook I know, and she has made a welcome dinner for you."

Eva proceeds to pull out an enormous tray of enchiladas. It's accompanied by rice and beans, guacamole, warm tortillas, and salsa on the table. The amount of food prompts me to ask, "Who else is joining us?"

Eva smiles. "It's just the four of us."

I don't think I can eat ten enchiladas, and the tray has at least forty-four by my count.

"Please, eat. I am sure you are hungry after the long journey. Army's brother, Juan, lives across the street and has asked us for drinks later, if you are not too tired."

We tuck into dinner and catch up on each other's lives, beginning with news of children, jobs, and grandchildren. We show them pictures of our newest grandson, Sam, and they glow as they talk about their kids at the university. Soon conversation turns to our plans for the stay. Though Army will have to work, Eva is sure he'll be able to get away and join us.

"We don't want to put you out if you guys have things to do," Karen answers.

Eva waves her hands. "No, it is fine. Please think about it and let us know."

I can't help myself. "I'd like to see the station where you work, Army. See how policing is done in Mexico." I avoid all eye contact with Karen at this point but feel her laser-beam eyes creating heat on my face.

"Yes, my friend, I would love to show it to you, but not for a little time yet. I want you to see the town and meet my family," Army says.

I'm a bit disappointed. I was hoping he'd be more excited to show me how policing is done here.

Dinner finished, I'm so full I can't chew another bite. Eva insists that Karen and I not help while she cleans up.

Army points out the bathroom off the kitchen before showing us to our room. The room is a soft green color with a single lightbulb hanging from wires in the middle of the ceiling. Two windows face the street, and a fabric blind and floor-length, white-laced, scalloped curtain hang in front of each one. The bed against the right wall looks rather small, maybe full-size at best.

Army remarks, "It's a honeymoon bed." Turning to look at him, I know he's blushing under that tan of his. I smile, aware of Army's quiet, devilish humor.

Karen replies, "I like it. I'm sure it'll be great." She begins to unpack the suitcases into the two large dressers situated opposite the bed.

Army and I settle into the living room. "Tell me about your adventure in Ireland. You solved two murders, I understand."

I lower my voice. "Well, not me so much as the unofficial detective I'm married to."

"So, did you find one or two murderers?"

"Two. It was a mess. There was a murder, then a suicide, or rather a murder to look like a suicide. Karen wasn't happy that I spent a great deal of time investigating the situation."

"Well, my friend, that will not be happening here. You and Karen are our guests, so you will relax and enjoy México!" Army smiles.

"Amen!" Karen's voice is suddenly present. Army and I both jump and laugh. Eva also enters the room, wiping her hands on a towel. "Are we ready to go to Juan's?"

Juan lives literally across the street from Army. The road is very dark without any traffic. No cars. No streetlights. But lots of stars.

When we arrive, Juan greets us at the door. "Welcome! Mi casa es su casa." His accent is slightly heavier. Like Army, he has deep brown eyes, but he's a few years older and half a head taller, making him about six feet tall. His black hair, flecked with grey, and slimmer build give him a businessman air. Army introduces Juan to Karen and me, then we follow Eva into a large living room with rich brown leather couches, matching chairs, and soft, warm lighting. On the center coffee table are salt-rimmed glasses with drinks that look like margaritas to me. Yum.

Juan picks up a glass and allows the salt to slide through his hand, most of which hits the table and floor. He isn't deterred and continues until we all have a glass. "This is a special Mexican drink, palomas."

Juan turns as a beautiful dark-haired woman enters the living room. "This is my wife, Carlota. She made some snacks for us." She is full-figured, the soft curls of her long hair falling around her shoulders. Her eyes are the color of milk chocolate. She places a platter piled with sliced beef, soft-shell tacos on the table. All I can think is that I'm so full, but I know it'd be rude to not eat at least one. Karen and I sit on one of the couches, and Eva and Army move to the other one, across from us. Juan and Carlota sit in the chairs. To be a good guest I plate one of the tacos. The first bite surprises me. The beef is delicious and perfectly seasoned. I finish it.

Juan leans back in the chair and flexes one foot in his shined black dress shoes. "What are your plans for tomorrow?"

"I'm not sure. If Army has something planned, then Karen and I'll tour our new hometown," I reply.

"Army, you are not going to the funeral? You are Comisario General, you need to show your support," Juan remarks.

Army flashes an angry look at him.

Old cop habits die hard. "I'm sorry, who died?"

"Ana María Mendoza, the wife of a local race car driver, José Luis Mendoza. They were involved in a terrible auto accident near the highway. Oddly, he suffered only a broken shoulder and is under investigation," Army replies before I can ask for the details.

Juan spats, "Do *not* start! Show respect. He is a great man from our hometown. This is a terrible accident."

Okay, the conversation is getting good, and my curiosity is piqued. Army gives me a look that I know all too well, that there's more to this story than we're being told. I decide to pick his brain later when Karen's not around.

To change the topic, but not really, I ask, "Is there professional car racing in Mexico?"

Juan looks stunned. "Sí, there is NASCAR México. It is very popular here, with many fans."

"A professional race car driver involved in a terrible auto accident that kills his wife and leaves him with minor injuries does seem . . . ironic, if it wasn't planned," I say.

Juan bolts upright. "Are all police detectives so quick to judge? José Luis worked hard to get where he is. Even after his injuries. My brother sees a crime when it is only a tragedy."

Karen's eyes flash a warning to stop as she pats my knee. I know I should, but my coppy senses, and my need to defend my friend, are stronger than my good sense. "I'm sorry if I offended you. You've been a great host. Please tell me more about José Luis. You said he'd come back after some injuries."

Juan's shoulders relax with a deep sigh. "Yes, when José drove in the K&N Pro series, which is below NASCAR here in México, he had a terrible accident on the track and suffered a ruptured disc in his neck, but he got strong and went on to NASCAR. Then he had another bad accident and again suffered injuries to his neck. Doctors told José that he could no longer race."

Karen interjects, "Oh, how sad for him."

Juan stands up and walks to a bookcase behind us. "I was there when he won his first race." He hands me a frame with a racing ticket. "It is a terrible loss to the sport."

Carlota's velvet voice interjects, "I spoke with Ana María a few days before the accident, and she said that José Luis was doing well and hoped to form his own racing group."

"That must be very expensive. Did he make that much

money racing, or was he using his fame to get investors?" I question. My eyes search between Juan and Army.

"Maybe both," Juan states. "Ana María was very rich. Her father sold most of his land for cash before he died and left everything to Ana María. Now another tragedy. José Luis needs support, *not* suspicion." He shoots Army an angry look.

Army shrugs his shoulders. I'm sure he doesn't want to start a family argument in front of guests.

Conversation settles into reminisces of childhood and working.

Later that night, curled together in bed, Karen speaks into my shoulder, "Listen, Detective. This is their country. This is their hero. This is their funeral."

My coppy sense smirks.

CHAPTER 2

The bleat of a goat wakes me. Or maybe it was a dream. With the second bleat, I know it's real. A goat. The room is completely dark. If I turn on the single overhead light, I'll wake Karen. In stealth mode, I slip out of bed, creep my way to the window, and pull back the room-darkening blind ever so slightly. The sun is in full vigor, and yes, there is a goat on the sidewalk beneath the window. Its body is tan and brown with a dark brown face and a long brown goatee. One horn points straight back and the other makes a ninety-degree angle to the left. The goat looks up at me, blinks his one blue eye, and bleats, or whatever that goat sound is. *Toto, we're not in Kansas anymore.* I can't help but smile. We're in Mexico on vacation. As our son used to say, "It's *'a aventure.'*"

Turning back from the window, my fully dilated eyes find the room darker than before and I have to fumble for my clothes. I find a shirt, but pants elude me.

A voice from the darkness playfully says, "Just turn the light on before you hurt yourself."

Karen is awake, totally deflating my illusion of possessing ninja-like skills. "Sorry, I was tryin' not to wake ya."

"It's all right. I'm awake. I had this weird dream that we

were at a funeral. A beautiful, young, blond-haired girl was lying in a glass coffin. A crowd of mourners were standing near the graveside and crying. Suddenly, a cloaked figure appeared, but he didn't have hands, they were claws. He pushed a man into the grave. People started screaming and running. Another man pointed to the figure, but when he spoke, it sounded like a goat bleating. That's when I woke up." Karen laughs more to herself.

"That is a weird dream. A goat of all things."

"Yeah, just a silly dream."

I find the light switch and turn it on, then suddenly wish I hadn't as I become completely blinded for an instant.

Karen says she'll join me in a few minutes. I finish dressing and make my way out through the living room and into the kitchen Army and Eva are at the kitchen table.

"Good morning," I call out.

"¡Buenos días! You are up early. How did you sleep?" Army asks.

"Good. Very good. I had a goat alarm clock."

Army shakes his head. "It belongs to my crazy neighbor, Jesús. His house is at the far end of this street. He keeps his goats in his garage at night instead of the nearby pasture, except for Ernesto, who lives in the house."

I knit my eyebrows together. "Why does he keep his goats in his garage?"

He sighs. "He says he is keeping them safe from the Chupacabra. But they escape and wander all over town, and then he calls the police to round them up and bring them back."

I'm confused. "What's he worried about?"

Army throws up his hands. "The Chupacabra! It means 'goat-sucker.' It's a folktale. A mysterious, three-clawed beast attacks livestock, especially goats, and drinks their blood. Anytime an animal, and even people, are killed or go missing, the Chupacabra gets blamed. In the past, I have been asked to organize a search for it. Never found anything."

"I take it you don't believe in it."

"I respect the old ways, but as you know, I have spent my adult life in policing. Facts make a case. Humans can be some of the most harmful animals on the planet. I want my officers to be more science-based in their policing, but it is hard. People cling to the things they know."

"This is one that you are not going to win, my darling." Eva taps him gently on the cheek. "You know my feelings. I think there are things that cannot always be explained with science."

A faint sound of a goat comes from somewhere outside.

Karen joins us at the table. "Good morning, all."

Eva serves us mugs of fresh coffee. When the smell hits my nose, I'm immediately calm. It means home and family to me. The first sip is strong and slightly more bitter than I'm used to, but it's good. Eva also places a platter of various sliced breads in the center of the table.

Karen lights up. "Those look delicious. Did you make them?"

Eva laughs. "No, there is a family-run bakery in town. They make all kinds of breads each day. Hopefully you will enjoy them. Please help yourself."

Karen hums and wiggles with delight as we share a slice. I feel the same. The bread melts in my mouth. Karen and I sample three different slices while Eva makes another pot of coffee and says something in Spanish to Army that I don't understand. But I do know the look Army gives her, and it's not good.

"Eva and I will need to attend the funeral of Ana María Mendoza. I am sorry, my friends," Army apologizes.

"No, please, Karen and I don't want to be a bother. You need to go. In fact, I'd be more than willing to go with you, if you'd like." I meet Karen's eyes and give her my best smile. Her eyes don't look happy. Maybe she's recalling her dream after the mention of the funeral.

Army doesn't miss a beat. "That would great. It will be a good way to meet many people, and then you can tell me what you think of them." Army is now avoiding Eva's stare. Some things cross international borders.

"That sounds like a plan," I say, hoping to lighten the palpable tension at the table. Breakfast finished, Karen and I return to our bedroom, but once the door is closed, she spins around to face me, her eyes narrow. "I don't think I brought a suitable outfit for a funeral. What are you up to?"

Aghast, I reply, "Nothing. I'm just supporting my old friend. I'm sure no one will even notice us."

"I'm sure we'll just blend in because there'll be a number of non-Spanish-speaking, middle-aged, white people from out of town there."

"That's what I was thinkin'."

Karen rolls her eyes. "Really, that's what you're going with? Army said he wants to hear your opinion of the people you meet. That sounds like you're going as a *profiler,* as in a *detective.*"

I shake my head. "No, I don't think that's what he had in mind."

"Uh-huh, sell it somewhere else, sister." Karen looks through her clothes and pulls out a pair of black dress pants and a deep green blouse. "I hope this will do," she states as she gathers her clothes and heads to the bathroom to take a shower.

If I end up investigating another crime while on vacation, it may be the last thing I do. Karen could blame it on the Chupacabra if I end up dead in a ditch or just plain 'missing' here in Mexico. I dismiss the thought and gather my clothes to take a shower when Karen is done. Army lets us know that we'll be leaving soon. His SUV will hold all four of us comfortably, at least physically. Emotions may be a little strained.

Showered, changed, and in Army's car heading to the funeral, everyone's quiet. It's a short drive from the house to the church on the other side of the village. The roads are dirt, gravel, and rutted the entire way. Dust flies behind us as we drive, and gravel clicks against the fenders. We double-park on the street near the front of the church. I guess the 'Chief' isn't worried about a ticket.

"I can't believe they are having the funeral in the new church," Army comments to Eva, who shakes her head solemnly.

I'm confused. I see a Baroque Catholic cathedral with grey concrete walls, double bell towers, a single centralized dome, and an eighteen-foot wooden door embellished with metal rivets. The church's cornerstone is engraved with the year 1896.

"Army, I thought you said this was the 'new' church?"

"Sí, our other church is much older," he replies.

Karen shrugs her shoulders at me.

I'm impressed at the longevity that this town has. This place was established when people in my hometown of Watson were nomads.

It's only the late morning, yet the day's heat has already begun to rise. The dark, cool, and quiet interior of the church offers some refuge. The combination of lemon oil and incense I smell brings me back to Sunday masses with my grandfather and fond memories. Army leads the way to a pew near the front occupied by Juan and Carlota. A sleek, black casket is draped with a blanket of red and white roses. The scent becomes overpowering as we draw near to it. We genuflect before sliding onto the kneeler to pray.

After a few minutes, I sit back and survey the church. In the front pew sits a young man, thirty-something, dressed in a black, pinstriped suit. The sling on his arm identifies him as the widower. There are two older couples, a set on each side of him. One of the women wrings her white lace handkerchief between her hands as she openly sobs. I assume they're the couple's parents. Slowly, people of all shapes, sizes, and ages crowd into the church.

Low and somber organ music begins to play. The priest enters from the side of the altar along with four altar boys, and everyone stands. I don't understand most of the Spanish during the service, but Karen and I follow the crowd on when to stand, sit, or kneel. People speak or do readings throughout the service, trudging from the congregation and climbing the steps to the pulpit, some twisting their hands, some mumbling, one of them staring out at us before beginning. I make a detailed inventory of the people there. Karen would accuse me of doing a threat assessment, and she'd be right. Many are elderly, but a few stand out. I notice one guy in the second row: curly hair, built like an offensive lineman. Who is he? Then there's the middle-aged man, black suit and even blacker eyes. We make eye contact, and all I see is anger. For what, I wonder? The death of a young woman, or that her husband survived? A particularly striking beauty in her early forties, five foot nine or so, shoulder-length blond hair, great figure and ample breasts, walks to the pew behind the widower and pushes her way to be right behind him. She doesn't take her eyes off him. Does she see an opportunity with the race car driver, or is it just a fantasy?

The final 'Amen' is spoken. We make our way to the car and follow the procession to the cemetery. The grass is brown and dry and crackles underfoot. How long has it been since it rained here?

At the gravesite, Karen and I stand further back, allowing for family and friends to be closer. Again, I don't understand everything that is being said, so I focus on the people. The young widower cries on and off throughout, as does one of the older women standing next to him. His mother or hers? There are close to a hundred people here, but most curious is a young woman, maybe late twenties, standing on a rise about two hundred feet from the grave. She has long, straight, black hair, and her abdomen is pressing fabric tight. Who is she, or better yet, who's the father of her baby? I'll have to ask Army if he knows.

The service must be ending as people walk away from the

grave. José Luis and his family remain for a few more minutes. Army and Eva join us at the car.

I lean over to Army. "Who's with the race car driver? What's his name again?"

"José Luis. That's his brother, Emilio, and his parents to the right."

I notice the brother, a taller, older version of José Luis. Emilio's grey suit is tailored to perfection. As he speaks, he's very close to José Luis' face, as if making a point. What could be so important that it needs this conversation now? My coppy senses are tingling.

"Army, what's the story with the brothers?"

"You noticed, huh? They are *not* friends. Emilio has said that his brother needs to get a 'real' job. Emilio is a local businessman, ruthless. He takes advantage of people not reading the paperwork he gives them. People have complained."

"And that's not illegal," I comment.

"No, it's not. Come, I will introduce you. I want to say my regrets to José Luis and the parents."

Emilio catches sight of Army, but not before José Luis slaps Emilio's hand away.

Emilio recovers quickly, and a smile appears on his face. "Hola, Comisario."

I understand the sentiment, however, the tone sounds condescending. Always gracious, Army shakes Emilio's hand, then turns to me. "I would like to introduce my old friend and partner, Daniel Novice." Emilio's grip is cold and clammy, and he squeezes a little too hard. I make sure I respond in kind. Emilio's hand and eyes drop before mine do. "Welcome."

"Thank you. I'm sorry for your loss," I say.

"Ah, yes, the loss. What can be done? I noticed you did not make it to Ana María's velorio," Emilio replies with a smirk.

Armando ignores the comment and speaks in Spanish to José Luis. I recognize that he's expressing condolences from the many times I accompanied him as he notified families in our years together. José Luis mumbles something I don't hear. Army pats him on the shoulder, then motions for us to leave. I follow him as he steps toward the Trailblazer.

Once there, I can't help myself. "What was that about? Does Emilio dislike you because you're chief? Do you think he had somethin' to do with José Luis' accident?"

"I am not sure about the accident, yet. He does not dislike me; he finds it amusing that I cannot bring charges against him."

"Because of all the people he's cheated?"

Army sighs. "Yes, my father included. Out of twenty acres of prime land for only five thousand dollars."

"Oh no! When?"

"Maybe nine or ten years ago, before I moved back. My father did not ask anyone's opinion before he sold. Emilio sold it to a developer for two hundred thousand dollars."

"What a piece of jerk! We gotta nail him for something!" I spit out.

Suddenly, angry voices can be heard coming from behind us, near the grave. Army runs toward the disturbance, and I'm right behind him.

Emilio is screaming at the young, pregnant girl. She refuses to make eye contact. Her head hangs down, her hair covering her face. She's holding her stomach.

Army puts himself between the girl and Emilio while I scan the crowd for trouble. Words fly between Army, Emilio, and Ana María's parents. Army signals for me. I stand next to the girl as Army states, "Necesito que te vayas." I've heard him say "You need to leave" many times. I gently touch the young girl's arm to steer her away from the family, and Eva and Karen join me. The girl relents. It's then that I notice her crying. Eva puts her arm around the girl's shoulders, walking with her toward the road while I join Army, but he has the situation under control. People are dispersing. Army surveys the area.

"We good?" I ask.

"Sí. Gracias. We can leave if you are ready."

"If you're sure."

Army and I back away. Eva and Karen are standing at the car, and I see the young girl walking in the distance. "Does she need a ride home or something . . . ?"

"No, she lives nearby."

The ride home seems twice as long and even quieter than the tense ride to the church. Arriving at Army and Eva's, Karen excuses herself to change. I stay outside, leaning against the house, enjoying the sunshine and rolling over everything I witnessed today. What's the story behind Emilio's business and the death of the wife of the race car driver, and does an unwed pregnancy play a role in any or all of it?

Army approaches me. "Are you and Karen okay, amigo? I am sorry about that scene." He snickers quietly. I look up and catch a slight grin on his face. He says, "But it was like old times. You and me in the middle of a family dispute."

A burst of laughter escapes my lips. "Yeah, we're fine. I'm curious why there wasn't an announcement of a lunch following the service. Does the family do something quietly?"

"Here in México, the family comes together to offer prayers, masses, novenas for the nine days after the dead are laid to rest. It is how we say goodbye. We offer prayers for the deceased to have a safe journey to God in the afterlife while we process our grief. They may have a gathering at the end of the nine days."

"What was Emilio saying about you not attending something?"

"Velorio. You would call it a 'wake.' Families have a viewing, usually at their home prior to the mass and burial. I know the family, but felt we were not that close. I left it for the people who knew and loved her the most."

Eva leans out the back door, calling us in for lunch. There appear to be a number of expectations of Army as family member, community leader, and a native son. I hope they don't conflict with his role as law enforcement.

CHAPTER 3

The late afternoon sun is starting to hide behind the houses. "Army, how about a walk?" I ask.

"That is a good idea, amigo."

Narrow, broken concrete sidewalks force the two of us to walk single file. Slowly, the sidewalk fades until there is only dry, cracked dirt. Row houses have given way to empty lots and finally open pastures. I say, "What was that all about at the funeral? Who's the girl, and what's the big deal?"

"The girl's name is Valeria Flores. She was saying that she was there only to offer her condolences to José Luis for the loss of his wife." Army sighs and kicks a stone down the street.

"So why was Emilio so angry?"

"The rumor is that she is pregnant by either José Luis or his older brother."

"Emilio? Well that puts a new spin on it. So, which of the brothers is it?"

"Valeria has not told anyone, as far as I know. Emilio said it was disrespectful for her to be there. I think he was trying to protect himself." Army shrugs.

"He could've been protecting his brother," I add.

Army stops walking and turns to face me. "No, Emilio

protects himself only. If José Luis is the father, Emilio would have stood there and enjoyed the embarrassment to his brother."

"What a dirty dog!" I snap.

"None of it is illegal. Immoral, yes. I will have to hope God has plans for him until I get him on something else." Army grins. I'd like to see justice served in this life first.

Our walk continues for several blocks. Dust rises with each step as my shoes scrape the gravel. Houses along the way fade as I'm lost in my thoughts from today's events, and I walk without watching where I'm going. A motorcycle buzzes by me and snaps me back.

Army laughs out loud. "Careful, my friend. This may seem like a sleepy little town, but drivers here are crazy."

"My fault, I wasn't paying attention. Normally I can pick up the sound of motorcycles when they're blocks away. I didn't hear anything just now."

"I remember your love of motorcycles. Do you still have all three of your bikes?"

"Yes, I do. Karen says that they're the other great love of my life."

"Motorcycles are cheap transportation here. Mild weather nearly year-round makes it easy for people to use them as their main vehicle."

"I can see that. Also, the narrow streets here must make it hard for two cars to get through. A cycle doesn't have that problem. Makes me jealous that I can only ride mine a few months a year."

"Yeah, but you ride responsibly. Even with all my years of policing, and as chief, I have had drivers pass me or even run up onto the sidewalks to get through." Army shakes his head.

"Well, I'm gonna keep my eyes and ears open for the different makes and models here in town. Hey, maybe we can ride together while I'm down here."

"That would be great, if you think that our wives will be okay with not coming. Many of the bikes here are not comfortable for two riders."

"We have three months to spend time together, sightseeing, eating, drinking, and relaxing. I'm sure Karen and Eva wouldn't deny us some guy time. It wouldn't be more than a couple of times with just you and me," I say, slapping Army on the back.

"That does sound like fun. I will see who has a couple of bikes *and* helmets for us to borrow, then we can make a plan."

"I noticed that not many people wear helmets. They're not required?"

Shaking his head, Army replies, "No, they are not. I do worry about people and the way they drive, but there is nothing I can do about it."

The road ends in front of a run-down, dirty, white stucco house. Moss creeps across much of the roof, and many of the windows have been covered with cardboard. What looks like a mangy Border Collie/German Shepherd/Chihuahua mix guards the front door. Several outbuildings are scattered nearby. However, what I really notice is the front door painted the ghastliest shade of electric blue.

"What's with that house, especially the door?" I ask.

Army huffs out a laugh. "Another one of the old ways. Blue doors are said to prevent any evil presence from entering the home."

He turns to start walking back to his house when a voice calls out. Army's body shudders. "No, no, no. He saw us."

"Who?" A man steps out from behind the blue front door, onto the porch, and moves toward us. He reminds me of a Mexican Robinson Crusoe. Tall, bone-skinny, beard and hair both shoulder-length. He is accompanied by the dog from the porch and the goat I saw outside my window.

"Crazy Jesús. The guy who thinks the Chupacabra is alive and well and living in the neighborhood," Army replies sarcastically.

"Oh, him."

"Sí, señor." Army turns toward Jesús, who goes on to explain something in Spanish. He makes sweeping arm movements, pointing over the hill and driving his index finger into the palm of his hand. I notice the dog and goat appear to be nodding in union with Jesús' explanation. I briefly entertain the idea of walking back home alone but think better of it. The only words Army interjects are "Sí, señor," and I recognize that this is Chief Army taking a citizen complaint. After what seems like forever, Jesús turns and wanders into the broken-down house, followed by the dog and goat.

I ask, "What was that about?"

"Jesús was reporting a crime. Last night, Ernesto alerted him to a sound, and they went to investigate. Jesús said that about a mile over the ridge, he and Ernesto saw men and trucks stealing several heads of cattle. He did not recognize anyone because he was too far away. I promised him I would look into it."

"Good thing Ernesto didn't start barking. It could have been very dangerous."

"Ernesto isn't the dog. It's the goat."

"The goat alerted him?"

"Yes! Jesús feels that he and Ernesto can communicate." Army raises his hands. "Welcome to my world."

When we arrive back home, I notice Karen and Eva have changed into jeans and tee shirts and are standing outside the house. Eva greets us. "Come, we are going to the zócalo for some fun and dinner."

I'm confused. "The what?"

"Zócalo, or plaza. In America, you call it a town square," she replies.

"I think it'll be fun after today's events," Karen interjects.

I ask, "Is something going on there?"

"Yes, it's like a church festival." Army states. "There will be music and vendors selling all kinds of things like tequila, food, and gifts."

"You had me at tequila. What are we waiting for?" I grab Karen's hand.

"I'm shocked, shocked I say, that you'd be interested in the tequila." Karen laughs, as does everyone else.

As we get closer to the plaza, I hear music and smell hot oil and chili powder. Turning the corner, I realize that it's a giant party. Streets have been blocked off. Dozens of vendors line both sides of the roads. Strings of lights in various colors decorate the booths. There's a raised platform at the end of one street with a five-piece mariachi band playing, the musicians wearing black suits with gold embroidery and matching large, wide-brimmed sombreros. People dance in the street to the sounds of the guitars, violins, and trumpets. Kids run through the crowds, laughing. Some people sit on folding chairs eating, listening to the music, or talking.

The joy is infectious, and I feel myself relaxing as all my senses are engaged. Karen and I hold hands as we walk. Ahead of us, Army and Eva do the same.

Army makes his way to a fresh fruit cart. I see watermelon, pineapple, mango, papaya, and several I don't recognize, all cut into strips. Army greets the vendor and points to a few, which are placed into a clear, plastic cup. Chili flakes and salt are sprinkled on them, and finally, fresh lime juice is squeezed over all of it. Army pays the man and hands me the cup. "This is how we do fruit in México. Try some." I take a piece that resembles a turnip or potato, but it tastes so much better. It's an amazing combination of sweet, crunchy, and wet. "That's really good. What is it?"

"Jicama. It's a root vegetable, but better. All of it's sprinkled with chili pequin flakes, coarse salt, and lime juice. This is comfort food for me. It's a taste from my childhood."

"It's wonderful." Spicy, smoky, salty, and citrusy combine in my mouth. Karen and I finish the cup as we continue our stroll through the square. I buy Karen and Eva palomas, while Army and I have cups of dark tequila añejo. Army makes his way to a roasted corn stand and orders four ears. He returns with roasted corn like I've never seen. "What's on these?"

Army laughs. "Mayo, salt, queso fresco, chili pequin, and lime juice. It's messy, but tastes out of this world." One bite and I know he's right.

"This is delicious. I never would have thought to combine these ingredients on roasted corn. What's it called?" I ask.

"Elote," Eva replies, "or 'Crazy Corn' is what my mother called it."

"It's great, but majorly messy. I'm gonna need several more napkins." Karen nods in agreement. I make my way back to the stand, then realize I'm being watched by a guy that I recognize from the funeral, the one who looks like an offensive lineman. He's leaning against the wall of a building, sipping a bottle of beer, and talking to several people. We make eye contact. He nods, and I return in kind. I pick up more napkins, but never fully take my eyes off him.

Once back with Army, I point out the guy. "Who is he? He looks like he could be dangerous."

Army nods to the man, who nods back. "That is our mayor and my cousin, Pedro Gómez. I am sure he would like to meet you."

I'm taken aback. "He's your cousin and the *mayor*?"

"Yep, I've known him all my life. He's a good guy!"

"He looks more like an enforcer for the cartel."

Army laughs out loud. "When you guys are finished with your corn, I will introduce you and Karen to him." It doesn't take us long to strip the cobs bare, wipe our hands, and follow Army across the street where he introduces us to Pedro. Even bigger up close, he smiles and extends a meaty hand that engulfs mine. "It is nice to meet you. I heard a report that friends from Armando's previous life are here in town. Welcome."

"Glad to be here, Mr. Mayor. This is my wife, Karen," I reply.

"Nice to meet you both. Please, call me Pedro. I hope you enjoy your stay in our town, and if you ever need anything, please let me know."

"That's very kind of you," Karen replies. "This fair is amazing."

"Thank you. I'm glad you are enjoying yourself. I hope it does not change."

My interest is piqued. "What would change it?"

"Change always happens. Sometimes good, sometimes not. I must look for ways to bring in money to support the town. Please excuse me—I see someone I must speak with." Pedro walks over to the black-suit man with the angry eyes I remember seeing at the funeral.

"Army, who's the guy talking to Pedro?"

"That is Juan Mercado. He's a surveyor from México City. Rumor has it he's down here scouting an area for a new water park that his company wants to build."

"He was at the funeral. We made eye contact, and from what I saw, he's not warm and fuzzy. What do you think about the water park?" I watch as Pedro and Juan are joined by Emilio.

"When I first heard the idea, I thought it was great. Jobs for the people here, a great place for the kids to hang out, and then maybe a source of revenue if it attracts people from a greater area. So, I did a little investigation into Perros Bastardos."

I try to translate the company name. "The company name is 'something' dogs. What's the full name?"

"Bastard Dogs." Army's eyes are without humor.

"What a terrible name for a company," Karen says. "Why would anyone pick that name, especially here in Mexico?"

"The founder and president of the company, Edgar Sanchez, was born in México, but his family moved to the United States when his father became a professor at Texas A&M University. Edgar chose to work in the oil fields and speculated on oil futures, apparently quite successfully."

"I still don't get why he chose *that* name for his company," I interject.

"Mr. Sanchez reported in an interview that no matter how successful he becomes in the U.S., he is always seen as a 'bastard' Mexican. I called a friend of mine who is a business attorney in México City and learned that Perros Bastardos negotiates tough contracts. They force local governments into selling land below market value and demand tax shelters while maintaining the greatest share of the profits. I get the feeling that the local governments are recouping less than they had hoped for."

"Then why do it?" Karen asks.

Army smiles. "We are poor, and some is better than none."

"So what's Emilio doing over there?" I ask.

"He has eighty acres he is hoping to sell in a prime location but will not budge on his price."

Eva breaks in. "Please, no more business talk. We are here to party!"

Army buys another round of drinks. We find four chairs near the band and sit and listen. Well, I don't really listen. Rather, I'm running scenarios through my head as to the implications this project may have on the character of village, increased crime, and political fighting. Who would win the most, and who stands to lose?

CHAPTER 4

Karen rolls over as I'm making my way toward the bedroom door. "What time is it?" she asks.

"Six a.m. I'm sorry, I didn't mean to wake you." Actually, I was hoping to avoid her this morning.

"Are Eva and Army up yet?"

"Army is. I'm going out to meet him."

"What do you mean 'meet him'?" Karen raises her head. "Daniel Novice, what are you up to?"

I realize I'm cornered. "Army asked me to ride along with him today. We'll be back in a little while. Go back to sleep." I head for the door and make a furtive grab for the doorknob, but I'm not quite fast enough.

"*Stop!*" Karen sits upright. "Army asked you to ride along while he goes grocery shopping or as an unofficial deputy? Trust me, there's a *right* answer here."

I lean my forehead on the closed door. "Less like the grocery shopping, more like the deputy."

Karen sighs. "I thought we talked about this."

I turn to face her. "I know, I know, but I was with Army when Jesús reported seeing some cattle rustlers two nights ago. He wants to follow up on it."

"Who's Jesús again?"

"The crazy farmer at the end of the block, who believes in the Chupacabra. Ernesto alerted Jesús, so they went to investigate and saw men loading someone's cattle into a trailer."

"Who's Ernesto?"

"Jesús' goat." I'm now acutely aware of how that sounds. It also doesn't slip past Karen, who laughs out loud. "Two of the finest detectives from the Watson Police Department are following up on a tip from a goat. I seriously don't know if I should be concerned that you're *both* doing this or just greatly amused."

"Har de har har. This is important to Army. It'll also give me some alone time with him. I won't be gone long."

Letting out a heavy sigh, Karen lies back down. "I wouldn't want to stand in the way of you investigating Ernesto's credible lead. Try and be back before lunch, please!"

Shaking my head and rolling my eyes, I step out of the bedroom. I'm positive I'm never going to live this one down.

Army waits at the back door with keys in hand. He's impressive-looking in his white uniform shirt with brass stars on the collar and his white Stetson. I smile. Sometimes the good guys really do wear white hats.

Once we're in the Trailblazer and heading out of town, Army tells me, "I think I know the place Jesús was talking about. It's a former agave plantation. The company went out of business and abandoned the land."

"Then whose cattle were stolen?"

"I am not sure."

"Did you get a report on it?"

"No, but that means the cows were grazing illegally. Without rain, many ranchers' fields are barren. They are moving livestock to anywhere that has grass available."

The more Army talks, the more my excitement grows. I can't admit this to Karen, but I'm ready to investigate my first cattle rustling.

Army turns onto a road that's little more than a path. The Trailblazer crests a small hill as gravel and dirt devils fly up in our wake, and the entrance to the plantation appears. The company name 'La Constancia' is painted on a wooden sign. Weatherworn, and the name barely visible, it dangles from a rusted chain on one corner of the entrance archway. We pull into what appears to be a fenced-in padlocked area. The wooden fencing is three tiers high, faded, stained and damaged in places. At the far end are several buildings.

Exiting the truck, I half spin, half leap, to avoid stepping on a cow pile. White tennis shoes are not the right policing gear.

Army laughs. "That is why I wear cowboy boots."

"Yeah, now ya tell me."

"Okay, you grab the camera from the back of the truck. I'll take notes as we walk through the general area. Hope for any kind of evidence to indicate who was here."

"A dropped wallet would be nice."

Army throws open his hands. "Or a lost car registration or license plate."

"We both know that ain't gonna happen, but it's fun working together again. We were a good team." I slap Army on the back.

"Sí, I miss working with you."

Dirt, gravel, and grass crunch under our feet. Several hundred yards in, I see the remains of the distillery, but more importantly, along the side of the building is a large metal container. "Hey, Army, what's that?"

After approaching the structure, he comments, "Someone has put in a makeshift watering trough. I will get the fingerprint kit. With any luck, I'll be able to pull some prints."

"Army, I see tire tracks in this pile of dried mud."

"That isn't mud, but those *are* tire tracks. While I print the trough, you make a cast of the tracks, and then we will try to hunt down the vehicle that made them."

"I'll trade you."

Army replies, "Sorry, I actually feel I have had enough crap in my life."

All I can think is that after more than thirty years in policing, this'll be a first.

From the back of the truck, Army pulls the fingerprint kit while I grab a bag of dry plaster mix and a couple gallon jugs of water. He hands me a bucket and a wooden stir stick. Good thing Army remembered water because the trough is nearly empty. We commence with our tasks and soon have our evidence: pictures, prints, and a cast of the tire marks.

We sit in the truck comparing notes.

"Well, I took a lot of pictures, and the mold of the tire tracks looks good," I say. "One of the tires has a cut in its tread."

"Thank you for that. I lifted several very clear prints. I will run them through my database when I get back into the office."

"This is just like old times. Remember that case back in Watson where we tracked those burglars through the snow?"

"Yes, my friend. That was some very fine detective work from both of us. Using hairspray on the suspects' footprints in the snow, then covering the tracks with red florescent fingerprint powder made them stand out." Army smiles.

"Yeah, but you were the master of the camera. Those pictures made the case," I reply.

"We are a good team." Army extends his fist, and I bump it with mine.

Looking at the cast, I remark, "I don't think these were made by a car or truck. Maybe a trailer? We'll know more once we have something to compare it to."

"Yeah, it may have been backed in to get closer to the cattle as they stood around the trough, or they may have been made when the cattle were dropped off. Jesús said he saw the truck head east. There is a slaughterhouse two towns over. How do you feel about taking a ride to see if we get lucky matching the tire prints?"

Before I can answer, Army's phone rings. "It's Eva."

"What time is it?" I ask.

"About 13:00."

"Tell Eva we're on our way. I promised Karen I'd be home for lunch."

"And this is your vacation." Army winks, lets Eva know we're en route, and puts the truck in gear. "Home it is."

Karen is sitting at the kitchen table as Army and I make our way through the back door. She smiles and shakes her head.

Army reads the situation. "Karen, I am sorry we were late. I kept Dan out at the scene too long."

She laughs. "You're a good friend. You're still lying for him."

"What do you mean 'still' lying?"

"Oh please. So many times back in Watson when you two were working late, I'd get a call from you explaining how you needed Dan's help with this or that. I knew you were making sure I wouldn't be angry with him."

"¡Dios mío! No comprendo." He shrugs and shakes his head.

Eva breaks in, "Everyone sit down. Lunch is ready."

I realize I'm starving. Army and I never had breakfast. It is all my favorite foods: rice, beans, guacamole, tortillas, and shredded chicken. Eva begins passing dishes, and I have some of everything offered. It all goes down easy.

"Armando, Sara called and invited us over tonight for coffee," Eva states. "Dan and Karen are to be her special guests."

Army doesn't lift his head. He simply nods and continues eating.

"That's very nice of her," Karen replies.

"The family is very interested to know who 'these people' are that are visiting from the U.S. You are like celebrities." Eva throws her head back and laughs.

Karen replies, "That's wonderful. I'm sure we'll have a great time."

"First, Dan and I need to run to the stockyard and look at some cattle," Army says, a smile lighting his face. "My brother-in-law, Victor, is interested in expanding his herd. It will not take long."

"Your brother-in-law is a cattle rancher?" I ask. "I didn't know that."

"Sí, my father left him the herd because Juan was not interested while my other brothers and I were living in the U.S. Victor has done a good job. He is very successful."

"Has he lost any cows to the rustlers?"

"Fifteen head just last month. He had been very fortunate up until then not losing any, but then the rustlers hit his herd."

"Then it's doubly important that we check out the stockyard . . . um, if it will help your family." I hope Karen doesn't notice my eagerness to go with Army. However, I'm not that lucky.

"Dan Novice, since when have you been interested in looking at beef that wasn't cut up and sitting on your plate?" Karen interjects, laughing.

"Since becoming Army and Eva's guest and helping the host family and . . . um . . ."

"Yeah, and there's nothing to investigate I'm sure. Nice try." Karen throws up her hands.

"I would feel better telling Victor that I am following up on a new lead," Army says. "We will be home in two hours, well, maybe three at the most."

Eva and Karen laugh. Army and I exchange a glance, not sure what's funny. Eva replies, "Fine, go. Be home by 6:00 p.m. I am sure that Sara will have a feast for us. I expect our husbands for tonight . . . no detectives. It is a party! Clear?"

We reply in unison, "¡Sí, señora!"

Once in the Trailblazer, I tell Army, "Spending the whole day working with you has been great. It feels like old times, but I promised Karen a vacation. Tomorrow I'm gonna look for tourist attractions in the area and plan something."

"You are right. Privately, Eva told me that we are not being good hosts. She already made plans for us to visit some ruins tomorrow. We were going to surprise you and Karen at breakfast."

"Perfect. I'll do my best to act surprised. Now I can focus on this investigation. This is great!"

"It is about an hour to the stockyards. I am not confident that the trailer will be there, but finding matching tire marks could help us know if the cattle are ending up here."

"Will anyone there be willing to talk to you?"

"I doubt it. I have not been successful up to now. The men there are tough. I may be a homegrown boy, but being Comisario General trumps all that."

"I won't be much help interviewing anyone, so I'll play stupid, hoping they'll ignore me while I have a look around. Any luck and we'll see the tire tracks."

Army agrees.

The state of the stockyard shocks me. It's a huge maze of fenced-in enclosures that are a total mess. Many of the railings are broken, with some missing altogether. The wooden posts have a severe lean problem. The white paint is all but gone, and what is left is splattered with feces, dried and not so. A dozen men in dirty tee shirts, jeans, and soiled boots stand in a group, some with cigarettes hanging from their lips. A few trucks are parked nearby, but no trailers.

The Trailblazer door opens, and I'm stopped by the stench. Cow manure, blood, and rotting flesh assault my nose. Army walks toward the men, but all eyes are on me. I make my way round the outside of the nearest enclosure. As I walk, I hear raised voices and glance at Army, who is shaking several hands. His body language appears confident, no distress. I relax some and peer into the yard, then up to the horizon, then down to the ground. Discerning one set of tire tracks from another while trying to appear disinterested.

I still have one eye on Army, not wanting to be too far from him if there's a problem. I stand on the bottom rail of the fence and look in one of the pens. Climbing off the rail, I then walk to the far side of the pen. I'm looking down when I hear shouting. "Oy! No!"

I make eye contact with one of the men. He signals for me to come back toward the group. Nodding, I turn and head for the truck, and then I see them. My coppy sense tells me that these are the tracks I'm looking for. There's a distinct cut on one of the tires. Hearing the men laughing, I shoot a glance at Army, but he's not amused. I lean down and pretend to tie my shoe, then mark the spot next to the tire mark and head to the truck. Army joins me in the cab.

"What was so funny?" I ask.

"Apparently me for thinking that anything illegal would happen here. You see anything?"

"I'm positive I found the tracks we saw at the old plantation. They're not in mud either. What do you want to do?"

Army rubs his hand across his chin several times. "For now, nothing. Let them think they fooled us. This place is privately owned. If I ask, I know I will not be allowed to make a cast of the tracks, and they will be gone before I can get back with a warrant. I have no legal cause to search here. Do you think you could find them again?"

"Absolutely! Are you thinking a late-night covert mission?"

"Not sure how legal it will be, but if the tracks match, I may have cause to stop any trailers on the road and cite possible equipment violations," Army replies.

"I like it. When are you thinking?"

"Tonight, after we get home from my sister's house and our wives go to sleep. But we should get home now. The women will be glad we are early."

"I'll use all the goodwill I can get at this point."

We arrive home with an hour to spare. Eva and Karen are sitting in the living room reading when we come into the house. Karen's eyes narrow. "Ummm, you're home early. That's nice. I was sure that at 6:15, I'd have to call and ask if you're on your way back. Are you two up to something?"

Army and I feign surprise. "I'm on vacation, remember?" I reply. "It would be rude to be late for a party in our honor. So here we are."

"Uh-huh. I'm not convinced, but I'm happy you're here. However, both of you need showers. It smells like cow dung."

CHAPTER 5

An hour later, the four of us are walking to Sara's. Army and I help Eva carry several dishes she has prepared for the party. The streets are deserted, eerily quiet, except for the occasional barking dog. Army turns left at the corner onto the main street in town, where streetlights illuminate a small business district that includes a grocery store, money exchange, and clothing store among several others. After two blocks, he makes another left. I suddenly stop, flashing back to various training scenarios: a pitch-black, narrow street, buildings close together on both sides, and the threat of shooters everywhere. I hear Karen's voice in my ear and feel her hand on my back. "Dan, what's wrong?"

"I'm not sure. It just feels tight, as if I'm being squeezed in this space," I respond.

"It's okay. Army would never put us in danger. It's just a street." She takes my hand.

Exhaling, I nod. "Sorry. Old habits."

We follow Army up the walk to a two-story stucco house. He lets himself in and calls out, "¡Hola!" The large living room is both warm and bright. A black leather sectional fills most of it, and a sixty-inch television occupies the far wall. A group of teenagers sits in front of it, playing video games.

An older female version of Army holds a plate of something that smells delicious. Army gives her a hug, then gestures to a gentleman standing nearby. "Dan and Karen, this is my brother-in-law, Victor Guerrero, and my sister, Sara."

Victor extends his hand. "Welcome to my home. It is nice to finally meet you. Please come in." His accent is very heavy, and I have to listen closely to understand. He's slightly shorter than I am, carries more weight around his stomach, and has his black hair slicked back.

We shake hands with both Victor and Sara while I use my limited Spanish. "¡Buenas tardes! Muchas gracias for the invitation." Victor knits his eyebrows together and sighs, but Sara jumps in, "¡De nada! We are glad you are here."

"Please come into the dining room," Victor says. Juan and Carlota are there. The room holds an ornately carved, dark brown, wooden table with chairs for twelve people. Sara indicates places for Karen and me to sit, and others fill in around us while Army proceeds to introduce them. Karen and I shake hands with everyone, but after the first six or seven people, I'm losing track of their name and relationship to Army.

The variety of foods smell even better than they look. Dishes are passed, plates are filled, and drinks are offered. Army hands me a water glass. "Tequila."

Conversation diminishes as we start eating. Victor says, "Dan, I hope you are enjoying your time here."

"Yes, it's been great. Everyone has been very nice," I reply. "I understand that you're a cattle rancher. That must be very hard work."

"Sí, I have done it most of my life. I started working for

Army's father when I was thirteen. He taught me everything I know about cattle."

"I imagine these cattle rustlings are hard on ranchers. Have you heard anything about who might be behind them?"

"No, I have not. I guess that is a mystery for my brother-in-law, the Comisario General, to solve," Victor replies. "Can I get you anything else? Please, eat more."

He seems quick to change the subject, but I can't let it go. "Really, no rumors of any kind? Isn't that unusual for a small town?"

Victor's eyes flash with anger. "I have *not* heard anything." Then he sits back in his chair, crosses his arms across his chest, and smiles. "Except for the Chupacabra. Is that not right, Armando?

I meet Army's smoldering eyes and get the feeling there's something going on here. He says, "One never knows who *or* what dark forces are at work. I know for myself that right now I will have more rice and beans." Army looks back at his plate. I sip my tequila and run possible scenarios of what's going on here.

Karen pats my arm. "I think that sounds interesting. We'd love to help. Wouldn't we, Dan?"

"I'm sorry, I wasn't listening. What are we helping with?" I ask.

"Sara was just saying that she and Eva are part of the town's Preservation Society, and they are planning to restore the town's only remaining Spanish hacienda to its original state. It sounds fascinating. Is it here in town?"

"Sí, it is about six blocks from Army's house," Sara states.

"Wow, that's close. Great. Karen and I will help in any way we can. When was it built?" I ask.

"We think it was around 1697," Sara says. "The Bonilla family has been the only owner."

"Why are they selling it now?"

Sara sighs. "It is very sad. The hacienda has been vacant for many years. The Society has been trying to buy it for the past five or six years. But Señor Bonilla was very sick and couldn't keep the place up. When he died, his only child, Ana María Mendoza, inherited it, but now she has died and her husband does not want it."

Ana María Mendoza. The wife of the race car driver. He's already selling off part of her inheritance. I'm curious what else he's doing, or maybe it's his brother Emilio's idea. I don't like the way Emilio treats people.

"Karen and I can hardly wait to be part of this," I reply.

Sara smiles. "Karen, Eva said that you have wonderful taste in interior design. I know you're on vacation, but would you be willing to research Spanish haciendas and give us some ideas?"

"I'd be honored. It sounds like fun. If there're other restored haciendas nearby, maybe Dan and I could visit them and see what they did."

"¡Muchas gracias! Thank you," Sara says, patting Karen's arm.

Victor breaks in, "Sara, enough! Dan and Karen are guests of Army and Eva. They are not here to work." His eyes hold no warmth. Sara drops her gaze and pushes food around her plate.

Karen cheerfully offers, "No, it's not work. I love doing stuff like this. Dan and I are great partners when we have a project. To tell you the truth, I can't wait to see the inside of the building. When can we get in?"

"Well, we do not officially sign the papers until next week Wednesday," Sara says.

"The current key holder is a friend of mine," Army says. "I will have him sneak you in before then, if that is okay?"

Karen replies, "Yes, that would be great. Sara, can you and Eva join me?"

Sara wiggles in place, and her chest swells with pride. "I run the local grocery store, but I can be there tomorrow in the morning for a short time."

"Thank you, my friend, for your willingness to help," Eva says.

I am happy for Karen. She does love interior design and the creative process. I'm curious to see if Emilio had something to do with this deal and if it was legal.

I know that I'm being a bad guest, but I inquire, "It seems strange to me that José Luis would be selling everything so soon." I look from face to face.

Sara replies, "I think owning the hacienda made him sad. Ana María was the person who suggested the Society buy and restore it. She gave us the money to get started."

"Really?" I say. "Then the terrible accident stopped all that. So then the price of the place went to José Luis. Think he will use the money to start his racing team?"

Sara's eyes flash anger. "I think he would *rather* have his beautiful wife."

"I'm sure you are right," I say, bowing my head. "Where did the accident happen?"

Victor cuts in dryly, "On the road near the mountain pass. There is a curve where it is hard to see other cars, and drivers are speed crazy." He looks at Army. "Maybe the policia should do something about that."

Without looking up from his plate, Army snaps, "If it *was* an accident."

Everyone jumps when Juan slaps his hand on the table. "*Enough*, Armando. It is a tragedy. Stop looking for una conspiración. Leave the man in peace to grieve his loss."

Army's face flushes with regret, so I try to take some of the pressure off him. "I'm sorry. I didn't mean to bring up a sad situation. I guess with all my years of policing, I'd want to find a way to not have something this terrible happen again. As a trained accident investigator, I could look at the place where it happened and possibly suggest improvements to avoid this in the future."

Army says, "We will talk later, Dan."

"I think this is a subject best dropped," Victor adds. "If you policia want to discuss it when alone, then fine. This is a celebration." His eyes are dark and foreboding.

Carlota changes the subject. "You are right, Victor. I just want to tell everyone that Juan and I want to host a cookout while Dan and Karen are here. Victor, can you supply the steaks?"

Victor changes his frown to a less-than-genuine smile. "Sí, you have never tasted beef as delicioso as mine."

"I will let everyone know when we have picked a date." Carlota beams as she looks at Victor.

Is she secretly interested in Victor? Or is it already going on?

Sara asks, "Karen, Dan, are there any places you want to explore while you are here?"

"Eva and I already discussed it. Tomorrow is all about Dan and Karen being tourists," Army says with a smile.

"Please, not if you have something else you need to do," Karen replies.

Army waves his hand. "No, we want to show you the Aztec ruins. I think you will enjoy it. It takes about two hours to get there, so if we leave early, then we have the whole day to explore. Okay?"

"That sounds fun. Thank you," Karen says.

Juan grunts. "Tourist trap."

Army stares at him. "I think they will like it. They are guests in my home, and I want them to have some enjoyment while they are here."

"Army, my friend, I'm sure it will be great," I add. "Thank you for doing this for us. You're a good man."

Conversation changes to things to see and do while here. Everyone seems to have an opinion, and I notice Karen making a list of the suggestions. I sit back in my chair, enjoying the possibilities and more tequila.

Laughter, food, and talk of hacienda renovations cause the hours of the evening to slip past. Soon we are stepping out into the late-night air. I feel invigorated.

Army pulls me aside and whispers, "Meet me in the kitchen after Karen falls asleep."

I wink acknowledgement.

Eva and Karen are a few steps ahead. Karen calls over her shoulder, "What are you two conspiring to do?"

"How to make the most out of this trip," I reply with a smidgen of guilty. Not a lie. Working with Army has been a fun part of being here. It feels natural.

Karen snorts a laugh. I catch up to her and take her hand. We quietly walk the rest of the way home.

Once in our room, Karen and I get ready for bed. I can't even pretend to be sleepy. After I've turned over several times, Karen says, "Get up and do whatever it is you and Army are planning. Just be safe."

Kissing her on the forehead, I roll out of bed. "Darn detective I live with," I mutter under my breath. Dressed and out of the bedroom, I meet Army as he's stepping out of his room.

"Ready?" he asks.

"Absolutely!" I reply, grinning. Once in the truck, we head for the stockyard.

Army shoots me a sideways glance. "You can remember where you saw the track?"

"Yes. When I found it, I pretended to tie my shoe and instead arranged four stones in a square next to the print, then counted my steps to the last fence post. If I reverse it, I should be able to find it."

As we approach the stockyard, Army turns off the headlights and slowly coasts the truck up the drive. At the entrance, we get out. Army turns on a flashlight and hands another one to me as we start walking. When we reach the fence post, I move to the left and start counting my steps, hoping I remember correctly.

I hold my breath and shine my light down. The stones are right where I left them, next to a tire print. I give Army a thumbs-up. He hands me the stir stick and gallon of water. The two of us work in silence, with him pouring the dry plaster into a bucket while I slowly add the water and mix until it's the right consistency to pour into the print.

Waiting for the mold to set takes longer than I remember. The night is clear, and the bright stars seem close enough to touch. Army taps my shoulder, and I pull up the hardened cast. Too dark to tell if it's a good print. I shrug my shoulders. Army nods and motions for us to start back toward the truck. I place my hand on the car door handle when suddenly there's several people yelling in Spanish. On the rise behind the stock pens, I see the beams of multiple flashlights.

Army swings open his door. "¡*Vámonos!*" He doesn't have to tell me twice. I'm not even sure my door is closed before Army starts the Blazer and puts it into reverse. He floors it as we fly down the driveway. I hear a shot fired. When he hits the pavement, Army barely slows down before shifting into drive and gassing it. We're racing down the road *away* from his house. Neither of us says anything for several miles.

In the dark, I hear Army snickering, then say, "I am way too old for this, but it was great!"

I laugh out loud. "Just like old times. Who do you think they were?"

"I am not sure. I didn't hear any cattle or other trucks. They may have been waiting for a delivery. For now, let's get home so we can have a look at the plaster cast. I hope it matches the other one. I am a patient man, and time will reveal all."

"I don't mean to sound skeptical, but you do know we're going the wrong way."

"I know another way home that does not take us past the stockyard." Even in the dark, I see a broad smile on Army's face.

CHAPTER 6

The next morning, the four of us are seated comfortably in the Trailblazer on our way to the ruins. I sit back and relax in the front seat while Army drives and listen to Eva and Karen discussing color palettes and looking at books Eva has on traditional Spanish haciendas. Dirt roads lead past small farms, rolling hills, various towns, and, at times, barren landscape. I am struck by the contrast between the stark beauty and abject poverty.

We make our way to a gravel lot and park. I step from the comfort of the truck into the intense sun and the already stifling heat. Individual vendors line the perimeter of the parking area. The smell of fresh baked goods lingers in the air, and colorful woven blankets, trinkets depicting the pyramids, straw hats, and tee shirts are displayed. We follow Army as he heads for the entrance, pays the admission fee for all of us, and speaks to an attendant, who points to a heavyset man with short, grey hair. Army motions us to follow him. "This guide speaks English so we will be in his tour group." He refuses my offer of money.

We approach a group of ten people surrounding the guide. "Welcome everyone," he says. "My name is Tomás, and I will be your guide. I will give a brief history, and if you have any questions, please ask me. There is a traditional Aztec market where you can buy clothes, jewelry, and water in plastic bottles." We laugh, and my eyes wander over the area. I'm struck by the beauty and vast size of this ancient site and deeply impressed by this accomplishment without modern tools or machinery.

Tomás continues, "The Aztec civilization was one of the most dominant indigenous societies in México and Central America until the Spanish conquest in the sixteenth century. They excelled in several areas. In agriculture, they grew corn, or, as we say, maize, as well as beans, squash, and other vegetables. Their astronomy used a complex system based on 365 days. Let us continue the tour."

We follow Tomás as he moves toward a stone structure that rises dramatically in front of us. Its massive and imposing presence causes us to tilt our heads back just to visually see the top. "As you can see, they were architects who built great stone structures, including this temple, the adjoining palaces, plazas, and even courts to play their ball games.

"What were the Aztecs known for?" I ask.

Tomás comments, "Researchers have found that they were innovative in their agricultural methods, including irrigation canals. If we could move a little further down, I want to point some things out."

The group follows Tomás until he stops in front of several stone columns. "Many columns are carved, depicting the natural gods of the sun, moon, rain, or corn. Animals and even demons can be represented here as well as rulers, family, and military victories, among other things."

Karen taps me on the arm. "We passed a restroom a while back. Can you stay around here so I don't get separated from you?"

"I'll be right here," I reply. Karen hurries off while Eva and Army wander over to the grassy ball court. Tomás is talking about the Aztecs playing a game that sounds like a cross between basketball and field hockey on this grassy open field. I'm in awe of the 'ancient' civilization that had a hierarchy, commerce, art, skilled trades, leisure activities, and strong sense of community. After about ten minutes, Karen rejoins the group. She appears upset. "You okay?" I whisper.

"I'm not sure," Karen replies. "On my way back here, I stopped to look at the snake carving on the stairs of the main temple, and when I turned around, there was someone dressed like a conquistador. He was holding his spear with both hands and blocking my path."

"Did he threaten you?" I reach for her arm.

"No, I didn't feel threatened. More like he was telling me something."

"Like what?"

"I thought maybe I did something wrong. He said, 'Beware the warrior. Maintain your guard, always.' I didn't know what he meant or what I was supposed to do."

"Then what?" I wonder if the soldier was in his play-acting mode, or if he was telling a person who he assumes is a tourist something important. Warning? Threat?

"A formation of other conquistadors was walking by, and he turned and stepped in line with them. They came around that corner and must have walked right past you. Didn't you see them?"

"No, and we've been standing here since you left. What do you think he meant?"

"I don't know what to think. I was more shocked then, but now I'm just confused. Anyway, let's just enjoy the rest of the day," Karen insists.

Tomás has finished the tour. He thanks us for our time and interest in the site, then wishes us an enjoyable day. We are free to continue to visit the grounds.

"I see several food carts," Army interjects as he reaches my side. "Let me buy you lunch. And we have drinks in the car, so we can have a Mexican picnic." I never pass up food. Eva and Karen head to the truck to get the drinks while Army and I stand in line for food. Corn husk-wrapped tamales. Army pays for twelve of them and hands me six to carry.

Just as we arrive at the truck, his phone rings. "Hola. Sí. ¿Qué? ¿Muerto?" My head pops up. I know that word. Dead. He continues, "No. ¡NO! No es Chupacabra. Solo asegure el area. Sí. Adiós." He closes his phone. "I am sorry, but I must get back. There has been a death."

"Who?" I ask.

"Juan Mercado, the surveyor for the proposed water park. He was found a short time ago."

"Did you say 'Chupacabra'?"

"Sí, Jesús was walking with Ernesto when they found the body. That stupid goat gets out more than most people I know. Jesús has convinced my deputy that the body has all the markings of an attack of the Chupacabra. I am sure Ernesto told him that."

I search Karen's face to be sure she is fine with my investigating a crime scene while on vacation. She laughs and nods. "Do you want some help at the crime scene?" I offer.

"Sure. I have asked the deputy to secure the area. I need to get back as fast as possible before evidence is lost, buried, blessed, or who knows what. I am so sorry, my friends. This was to be a fun day, and now it is ruined."

"No, it's not ruined," Karen says. "We thank you very much for today. It's been fun."

"Yeah, we saw the ruins, Karen was accosted by a conquistador, and now there's a case. But let's go, time's a wastin,'" I add.

Eva places her hand on Karen's arm. "Accosted by a conquistador? What do you mean? Are you all right?"

"I'm fine. It was less of being accosted and more being caught by surprise. I'm sure it was just someone role-playing here at the ruins." Karen laughs.

"Role-playing? They do not do that here," Eva insists. "Money is very limited. There are only tour guides and researchers."

Karen and I exchange a shocked look. If it wasn't someone hired to role-play, then who was it, and was Karen in danger? I have an uneasy feeling that the encounter could have ended much worse. It's little comfort to me that it didn't. All I know for sure is that I wasn't there when Karen might have needed me.

We grab the tamales to eat in the car and head back. Army is driving at quite a clip, which feels like old times. I miss going red lights and siren.

We quickly stop at the house. I help Eva and Karen unload

the Trailblazer while Army changes into his uniform and picks up his gun. Then Army and I drive out to the crime scene.

Army pulls up behind a solitary police car. A barren field extends in all directions, covered with grass the color and texture of straw. Stepping out of the truck, I look at the gravel road, which is more like a wide path, bone-dry. Dirt clouds kick up with every step. Ironic place for a water park.

Army makes his way to where a young deputy is standing, talking to Jesús and writing in a notebook. He's the only officer present. A perimeter appears to have been established and the scene secured; however, Ernesto continues to meander, chomping at the grass. I hope he doesn't eat anything that could be evidence. Jesús is speaking and making slashing arm movements. I can figure out what he's demonstrating.

I wander over to the body of Juan Mercado. He's wearing what's left of a short-sleeve cotton dress shirt, khaki pants, and brown loafers, but no socks. His head is nearly severed; his throat and chest are shredded with three deep cuts running horizontally across the body. What's curious is the lack of blood. The dirt and grass should be soaked, but there is hardly anything, not even pools that would've coagulated on the dust before they started to dry.

Army joins me. "What do you think happened?"

I can't resist a giant grin, a smart-ass remark on my tongue.

Army puts up his index finger. "You say 'Chupacabra,' and I will pull my gun out and shoot you myself."

I repress the comment. "Well, I don't think he was killed here. There's almost no blood. Whatever killed him left deep, curved cuts in three simultaneous rows. Is there a piece of farm equipment with that shape?"

Army shakes his head. "Nothing I can think of. Hopefully the medical examiner will be able to figure out what killed him. If he was not killed here, then where? And more importantly, why? Someone got very close to him."

"So, either he knew his killer, or they surprised him. The other problem is that the area is so dry, there aren't tire marks, footprints, or any useful impressions of any kind. I do notice that the grass looks like it has two faint trails. I think the body may have been dragged here from the road. Last I heard, the Chupacabra doesn't drive."

Jesús starts yelling from where he's standing, "Sí, es Chupacabra, sí!"

Army closes his eyes and sighs. "Dios mío, give me strength."

"Sorry 'bout that."

"I may still shoot you, but for now, can you work with my deputy, Diego, to process the scene? I'm going to walk around and see if there is anything else in the area that might give us a clue."

"I don't speak fluent Spanish, remember."

"That is okay. Diego speaks English. He was born and raised in California until he was fifteen, when his parents moved back here. Diego, come here." Diego steps toward us. He is a dark-eyed, dark-haired, twenty-something. Tall and lean. I shake his hand while Army does the introductions. "Diego, Dan. Dan, Diego. Follow Dan's lead and learn. There are gloves, a camera, and an evidence kit in the truck. Can you start by eliminating Jesús and Ernesto?"

"I gotta say, that's a first in my career. I've never had to eliminate a goat from an inquiry," I say.

Army shakes his head. "You do not have to actually print Ernesto, but we need him to stop moving around the scene and eating potential evidence. I will talk to Jesús about it. Welcome to my world."

"Okay. I can do that. I'll see if I can establish a time of death, too."

Diego photographs the body and surrounding area from all angles. I pull out gloves and the evidence kit and place paper bags on the victim's hands, securing them around the wrists. His pockets are emptied: coins, keys, and a strange-looking business card. Each is placed in its own evidence bag, noting where it was found. Wounds are individually swabbed for particulates, and each swab is placed in a separate labeled envelope. Opening the victim's wallet, I find identification indicating that this was Juan Mercado, and then I bag the complete wallet and contents. I roll the body over to check for lividity and find some pooling. Manipulating the decedent's arm up and down and his hand back and forth at the wrist, I find no signs of rigor. I can get a tentative window for time of death.

While Diego and I are finishing up at the scene, Army returns to tell us, "The M.E.'s van is on its way. After the body is removed, finish processing the scene. More pictures, soil samples, etc."

"Sure, Comisario," Diego blurts out.

I look at Army. "Me, too . . . Comisario." Army narrows his eyes at me and smirks.

The attendants arrive, speaking in short, clipped statements to Army. Army nods. They bag the body and load it into a plain white van. After they're gone, Diego and I finish processing the area.

After we're done, Army says, "Load everything in the back of truck. I'll take it home. I do not feel like going into the office tonight."

My head snaps up. "Are you sure? What about the chain of evidence process?"

"Yes, I'm sure. I will retain custody, and it is only one night."

I open my mouth to protest, then close it. I don't agree, and it makes me uneasy, but it's not my investigation.

Army motions for Diego to place all the evidence in the Trailblazer, then he releases Jesús and Ernesto from any further interviews, for now, at least.

Diego drives away in his squad car while Army and I climb into his truck. "Juan couldn't have been dead for much more than two hours," I say. "*Rigor mortis* hasn't set in."

"It was fairly warm today, so it takes longer for the body to cool," Army remarks as he puts the Trailblazer in gear.

"Yeah, but even then, it's six o'clock now, and the sun's been up for at least ten or eleven hours, so he was either killed indoors or somewhere very secluded. If he was killed in seclusion, why move him? I'll bet he was killed indoors and needed to be moved."

"What are you thinking? A crime of passion?"

I cock my head to one side, staring into the distance. My mind is racing, turning over theory after theory. "I'm not sure. Too many of the puzzle pieces are still missing."

Army ponders, watching the road.

I can't resist. "And then there's Ernesto's testimony. Does he have to raise his hoof when being sworn in?"

A low chuckle escapes Army's lips. "Let us get home and have dinner with our wives. We can review the evidence tomorrow." We ride the rest of the way home in silence as dusk settles on the horizon. I can't stop the thought that there is something else motivating Army's actions. Is there too much 'family' here?

When we come through the back door, Eva and Karen are at the kitchen table. Eva hugs Army and says, "You two must be starved. Sit down, and I will bring everything out. I have rolls, sliced meats, cheeses, and tomatoes. There is also fresh-cut watermelon and papaya. I hope that is okay?"

"It sounds wonderful, especially with a shot or two of tequila," I reply.

Army laughs. "That, my friend, I have. How does añejo sound?"

"Perfect!"

We eat dinner in relative silence until Karen asks, "You two okay?"

"Yes, but it never gets easier," Army responds. "I have to try and notify his next of kin. That is one part of the job I will always hate. I am sorry. I do not mean to ruin the evening."

Karen jumps back in, "No, you're not ruining the evening. I feel better knowing you and Dan still have kind hearts after everything you've seen in your careers."

"I agree with Karen," Eva interjects as she picks up our empty plates.

Army smiles. "Well, thank you. Excuse me." He stands up and heads into the bedroom to call the victim's family.

We settle in to watch a movie for the rest of the evening, then all head to bed. My mind is racing: murder, no blood at the scene, so he was killed somewhere else. I fall into a restless sleep when I'm startled awake by yelling. I pop up and head into the living room. Army's shouting and running out the back door. "*Detener! Policia!*"

I'm right behind him. The outside lights are off, and it's really dark. Army stops suddenly, causing me to run into him. Standing in front of me, he blocks my view. "What's happening?" I ask.

"Someone was breaking into the house!"

The person flees into the darkness by the time we reach the back of the yard.

"Dios mío. What is going on? First a murder, now this."

"Crap, the evidence!" I say. Army and I scramble back inside.

Eva and Karen are at the door. Karen asks, "What happened? We heard Army yelling. Are you two okay?"

"Yeah. Army heard someone breaking into the house. I'm not sure if they're after the evidence or just whatever they could find to steal."

We head into the living room and check each item against the evidence log. It's all there.

"Did you get a good look at him?" Karen asks.

"No, I didn't," Army replies. "He was average height, average weight, and wearing dark clothing."

Karen hesitates. "That's . . . not much to go on. Do you think someone was after the evidence?"

"This is just too coincidental. How did anyone even know it was here?" I search Army's face for a better explanation.

He sighs and shrugs. "I will put the evidence in the guest room and sleep there for the rest of the night. What time is it anyway?"

"Three a.m.," we say in unison.

CHAPTER 7

I'm up before the sun and check on Army. He's at the kitchen table drinking coffee. "Did you sleep at all?" I pour myself a cup and sit next to him.

"Not very well. Every little noise convinced me that someone was trying to break in again."

"What's our next move?" I ask.

"No, amigo, this is not *our* case. This is *your* vacation. I do not want Karen to kill you, or worse . . . kill me."

"I heard that!" Karen interjects from the doorway. Army and I both jump while she laughs. "I like a healthy level of fear in the men in my life."

Army puts up his hands. "Karen, I do not want to ruin your vacation over this."

She sighs. "I'm just kidding, Army. You and Dan are a great team. Always have been. If Dan isn't part of the investigation, he'll be thinking about it and won't really be with me no matter what we're doing. Then he'll know that I know that he knows that I know that his mind is on the case."

"This is one of the reasons I love her. She's a cop's wife," I say.

Karen gives me a hug and a kiss on the neck. "There's that.

Also, Eva, Sara, and I want to scope out the hacienda today. Army, can you get us in?" she asks.

"I will make it happen, and thank you."

"Great! We'll walk over there after breakfast." Karen claps. "I'm going to take a shower now."

Eva joins us at the table. "Anyone interested in breakfast? I could make eggs with sausage."

"Sure," I say, "but can we start with the leftover guac and chips? Army, you remember breakfast back in Watson after working all night on a case?"

"Sí, amigo. Habaneros' Restaurante. The manager, Alfredo, was always very kind to us. Guacamole, chips, enchiladas, and cerveza, then home to sleep for a few hours and back to work. We did a hell of a job."

"Yes, we did. We're gonna kick this one in the butt and get it solved," I reply.

Eva breaks in. "I do not mean to break up the bromance, but we would like to get into the hacienda around nine this morning?"

"Sí, mi amor. Anything for you," Army says.

Eva's deep brown eyes dance as she laughs and pats his arm. She pulls out the guacamole and chips and makes fresh coffee. Army and I dig in while she finishes with the eggs, sausage, rice, and beans. When breakfast is cleaned up, we take turns showering and getting ready.

"I made a phone call to the hacienda's key holder, Antonio," Army tells Karen. "He will meet you and Eva at the house at nine."

Karen nods. "Dan, I plan on using our camera today. Is the battery charged, and do we have an empty chip for it?"

"Yep, it's all set. I double-checked it while you were in the shower." I give her a kiss on the head. "Thank you, again."

"Yeah, yeah. Go have a good time, play nice, and stay safe. Just remember I want to have a vacation at some point."

I look her in the eyes. "We will. I promise." I know this case will end, at least I hope so. Karen has a list of places to see here. I owe it to her to make it happen.

Army and I pack up the evidence. One of the plastic bags slips out of my hand, but Karen reaches down and picks it up. "What's this? It looks like a business card, but it's nearly blank. What's that about?"

"I'm not sure. I didn't have time to look at it before I bagged it," I reply. It's glossy white with a tiny, black, embossed symbol in the upper right-hand corner. "Karen, does that look like a bird or something?"

Karen holds it close to her eyes. "It looks like a conquistador's helmet, but it's so small. There's nothing else on the card. No name or phone number, nothing. That's weird. Twice in one day there's been a reference to a conquistador."

"What would you use a card like this for if it doesn't have any information on it?"

"Secret society?" Karen replies. "You know, for members to identify themselves."

"What about a warning? Conquistador means 'one who conquers.' Historically, they were thieves, rapists, murderers, and looters," Eva adds.

"True. The man's dead. Maybe he didn't heed the warning and paid the price," I say. "How do we find out who the card belongs to?"

Army breaks in, "After last night, I may begin to believe in conspiracy theories. The card will be processed for fingerprints."

We pack all the evidence into the Trailblazer, and Army and I head for the police department. While driving, he explains, "After we properly secure the evidence, I want to check in with the medical examiner to see when he will finish the autopsy."

"Sounds good. How about we set up a murder board? I can photograph all the evidence and add it to the pictures from the scene."

"Good idea, and after everything is catalogued and photographed, we can run the evidence to the lab in Guadalajara."

The station is less than two miles from Army's house. The parking lot in front is nothing more than a dirt pad interspersed with broken pieces of asphalt the width of two cars. The building is a single-floor, grey-colored adobe brick. Black wrought iron bars cover every window, and a steel door showcases an impressive set of locks.

We carry everything in and check items against the inventory, then I start photographing. Army downloads the photos from the police camera and my phone onto his computer and prints them out. We lay the pictures out on his desk and decide which items will be affixed to the large dry-erase board: photos of the deceased, his wounds, and the surrounding area, as well as the business card. When we're finished, I step back from the board. "What we're missing is a motive and a list of suspects. You have any idea who'd want Juan Mercado dead or why?"

Army folds his arms across his chest, shaking his head. "I spoke with the medical examiner, and he will be done in a couple of hours. We should speak with the mayor and see if he is getting any opposition to the proposed water park. Disgruntled farmers, landowners, whoever."

I can't help myself. "Psychic goats?"

"Do not start." Army laughs, grabbing his keys. "How about we talk to the mayor now?"

"Will he be able to see us on short notice?" I ask.

"Yes. Murder is bad for the town, and if there is an issue, I will tell my aunt, his mother, and then there will not be a problem."

Army's family connection to the mayor's office could be a mixed blessing.

Army secures the evidence in a locker, then engages multiple locks on the office door. We walk two buildings over. Approaching the mayor's office, I hear angry voices coming from an open window on the street side of the building, but it's all in Spanish and spoken very fast. Army stops.

"What are they saying?" I ask. Army holds up his hand. He's listening. I'm listening too, but I don't recognize the voice. I'm only catching words here and there: 'prometiste,' 'dinero,' 'Juan Mercado' 'muerte.'" In my mind, that translates into 'You promised money in Juan Mercado's death;' however, I did miss several words in between. I can't hear Pedro's response. The next sound is a slamming door. Emilio Mendoza exits the building, nearly running into Army.

"Hola, Emilio. ¿Cómo estás?" Army asks.

He spits, "¡Sal de mi maldito camino!" then stomps to his car.

Army looks back at me. "He says, 'Have a nice day.'"

"Are you sure? Because I translated it into 'Get the fuck out of my way,'" I reply.

"You could be right, Dan. All the time I spent in the U.S., my Spanish is a little rusty." Army laughs and heads into the building.

I tap Army's arm. "Could you hear what Emilio and the mayor were talking about when we walked up?"

He shakes his head. "Not all of it. I do not want to speculate until I hear what Pedro has to say." He knocks on the door of the mayor's office and steps into the room.

Pedro is sitting behind an ornately carved wooden desk situated on the right side of the room. Two well-worn wooden chairs are in front of the desk. A map of the state hangs on the wall opposite Pedro's desk, and below it is a threadbare couch pushed against a wall. The floors are a deep brown wood with distinct wear patterns from the door to in front of the desk and behind it. The room is warm and moist. A ceiling fan does little to dispel the feeling. Pedro smiles, stands, and extends his hand to both Army and me.

"Hola. Let me guess why you are here. You want to know if anyone had a problem with Juan Mercado and the water park. Am I right?"

"Sí, and what did Emilio Mendoza want?" Army asks.

"He is still angry about the Town Council's decision on the placement of the water park. He insists he has a better piece of land and, with Mr. Mercado's death, that negotiations should be reopened. So, we disagreed." Pedro stands and grabs his suitcoat from the back of his chair. "Nothing to worry about. Please excuse me. I have another appointment."

Our meeting is apparently over, and I shake Pedro's hand. As Army moves in for his own handshake, he whispers something in Spanish to Pedro. Pedro's eyes are black and humorless, but a forced smile crosses his lips. He replies, "Sí." Army opens the door and walks out. I follow behind him.

Once on the street, walking back to the station, Army turns to me. "He knows more than he is saying."

"Yeah, you're right. Do you think he's protecting someone?"

"I am not sure at this point, but I am willing to wait and see what happens."

"What did you say to him as we were leaving?"

Army waves a hand dismissively. "A message for his mom. Nothing important. We can take the evidence to the lab in Guadalajara and, on the way back, stop at the medical examiner's office."

I don't fully believe Army, but consider that this may be a very delicate situation for him to navigate due to dealing with family. I decide to let it drop for now. "Okay. Should we let our wives know what we're up to?" I ask.

"We can stop in at the hacienda."

We pack the evidence into the Trailblazer, and after a short drive, we find Eva and Sara in the center courtyard, each with a pad of paper and pen in hand, while Karen is poised with the camera.

"Well hello, you two. Have you solved the murder already?" Karen asks.

"We're good detectives, but not *that* good," I say, laughing. "No, we're gonna take the evidence to Guadalajara, so we'll be gone for a few hours. You need anything before we take off?"

"Now that you mention it, they have a wonderful library there. I think we have done as much as we can here. Could Karen and I get a ride?" Eva asks.

Army nods. "Sure. We can drop you off then pick you up when we're done at the medical examiner's office, if that is okay?"

"Perfect," Eva replies. Sara informs us that she needs to get back to the store, and Karen and Eva climb into the back seat of the truck.

"How did your first look at the hacienda go?" I ask.

"It was great," Karen says. "It was first built in 1697. The outside stucco walls and hand-formed terrace roof are beautiful, but the inside must have been amazing."

Eva adds, "Yes, it has triple Romanesque arches that define each of the four sides of the courtyard, then the three-tiered fountain in the center."

"Oh, *and* all the details must have been made by hand," Karen replies.

Eva nods enthusiastically. "I can hardly wait to see if we can have the metalwork recreated. The biggest problem will be the roof, both in cost and in the need to have authentic materials."

I turn around to face Karen. "Where's the money for that going to come from?"

"Alejo Guerrero. He has volunteered to pay for a new roof," Eva says.

"That's nice." I think my mouth hung open for a second or two. "Is he another brother of Victor's?"

"Yes, Alejo is younger. Then there is the youngest brother,

Antonio, who is studying at the university," Eva states. "Alejo is arrogant. All he talks about is his degree in Spanish history from a university in Madrid, how his wife is from one of the oldest families in Spain, and what a great country it is. I think he has forgotten that Spain invaded México and raped and pillaged it." Her eyes flash with anger.

Laughing, I add, "He sounds like a horse's ass."

"Yeah, but if he's footing the bill for the roof, I can live with his attitude, even if he is an odd duck," Karen comments.

Before I can ask what she means, Army breaks in, "What are you looking for at the library?"

"Much of the original interior has been lost, so we are looking for ideas to recreate the feeling of when it was built," Eva says.

Eva and Karen quietly discuss the photos and notes from today while my mind drifts to murder. More specifically, the victim: why him and why now? I make my own list of questions that need to be asked and to whom. After more than an hour, Army pulls over at the Biblioteca Central. Karen and Eva get out of the car after kisses are bestowed to the appropriate spouse.

CHAPTER 8

We take a ten-minute drive, turn onto a very busy street, and pull into a small parking lot at the rear of a tangerine-colored cement block building. It's at the end of a row of different-hued structures. Walking up to the building, I notice three black hearses and nudge Army. "Busy place, huh?"

He nods. "Unfortunately." He pulls open a heavy metal door, and we head down a corridor.

"On to the crime lab," Army declares. I nod in agreement.

Crime labs smell the same in any culture: a mixture of coffee, antiseptic, and floral air freshener.

Army introduces me to several of the techs, including the receptionist, who reports, "Dr. Rodriguez sent up some trace evidence and the victim's clothes for processing."

"Dése prisa, por favor," Army states. She nods her head. He asked for a rush on processing the evidence.

"Okay, we can head over to the morgue and see if the coroner has found anything." Army points back to the corridor.

We walk into the autopsy room. The smell catches in the back of my throat: stale refrigerator meets iron-thick blood. Four stainless steel autopsy tables spike out from a center point in the middle of the bright room, each with individual overhead lights. Cabinets of equipment line the wall space. A bear of a man wearing a lab coat, as wide as he is tall, looks up and smiles. "Ahh, mi amigo. ¿Cómo estás?"

"¡Buenas tardes! Let me introduce you to an old friend and my former partner from the U.S., Dan Novice. This is Dr. Luis Rodriguez, the medical examiner for the state of Jalisco." When we shake hands, his engulfs mine, and I wonder how he fits them both into a body during an exam. "Pleased to meet you, Dr. Rodriguez."

"Call me Luis." I'm silently grateful that Luis speaks English.

"Anything on my victim, Juan Mercado?" Army asks.

"Well, yes. I have cause of death," Luis says. "He was garroted. Spinal cord was cut. His head was nearly severed. I found a fragment of a fine wire and sent it to the lab to be analyzed."

"What about the cuts on the body?" I ask.

"Postmortem. Done to either disguise cause of death or throw suspicion on someone else. The odd thing is that whatever the weapon was, it was shaped like a paw with three claws."

I'm confused. "What do you mean?"

"I measured the depth and width of the cuts. All had a very pointed end, but were rounded on the sides and are the same distance apart. I have only seen these types of wounds on victims of cougar attacks. However, the cuts here are much wider and deeper."

Army and I exchange glances. Luis hands Army the report. He scans the first page. "So, having strangled the victim, someone went to the trouble of slashing him with some kind of three-clawed weapon?"

Luis nods. "Looks that way to me. However, I cannot find a single weapon that matches the wounds. The lab did a 3D rendering from the measurements of the wounds." Luis hands the photo to Army, which shows three large animal claws adhered to a handle.

I have to ask, "What animal has claws that big? A lion or a tiger or a bear?"

"Oh my!" Army and Luis respond in unison. Smirks flick across both their mouths. I can't help but laugh.

"Seriously, if I had to guess, I would say that the claws were carved from a bone or an antler and then secured to a handle," Luis says. "I did find a particulate in one of the claw marks, which is at the lab for analysis."

"Gracias. Anything else?" Army asks.

"No alcohol in his system. Drug screen will be back in a few weeks. He was alive when strangled. No other trauma to the body. Nothing under his fingernails, but hopefully his clothes have something useful. They are covered in blood, dirt, gravel, and other foreign materials. If we get lucky, the person was injured in the attack and left something behind to identify him or her. I will let you know as soon as I have the results."

I ask, "Given the wounds, would a woman be able to do this?"

Luis nods. "Sí, if the victim was surprised or under the influence. The weapon does not take a great deal of strength, but rather swiftness and determination. One thing to note is that sometimes with a garrote, it can cut the murderer's hands as well, if the victim is struggling. Again, if we are lucky."

"Muchas gracias, amigo. You have done a wonderful job, as always," Army remarks, shaking Luis' hand. "We need to get together for something other than a dead body. Maybe drinks. I will call you."

"Sí, I look forward to that. Adiós. Vaya con Dios, amigo," Luis replies.

Extending my hand, I say, "It was nice meeting you, Luis."

Back in the truck, we discuss the situation.

"Garroting is a very up close and personal way to kill, so who would know Juan Mercado enough to do this?" Army speculates.

"Or who was angry enough?" I add. "Garroting is personal, but very silent. Maybe it wasn't personal but necessary."

"Somewhere a gunshot or scream would be heard. It supports the idea that he was killed somewhere else and moved." Army drums his fingertips on the steering wheel. I can almost see him moving the pieces of the puzzle around in his brain, looking for connections.

"Yeah, but we still don't know where," I say. "Well, maybe the lab will find something. Time will tell."

Army calls Eva, and we head over to the library to pick up our wives. They are waiting outside when we arrive. Prior to climbing into the truck, Karen hands me several books on Spanish architecture. "I don't understand all the written language, but the pictures and drawings are wonderful. I can't wait until we get to Eva and Army's. Eva has some wonderful ideas."

"Then it was a successful trip for everyone." I hand the books back to her. "I'll have to bring you up to speed on our investigation."

Army snaps, "*No!* Not yet. We still have a great deal to do."

I'm taken aback by his uncharacteristically sharp tone. Karen's head snaps up. After an awkward pause, she jumps in, "I think Eva and I will be working tonight after dinner." They begin discussing the next step in the renovations. The air between Army and me is quiet the entire ride home. I'm trying to understand the pressure he is under and be supportive, if that is what's behind this. Maybe I need to give him some space in this situation.

Once we're back at the house, I offer to carry the books inside for Karen. "No, thank you. We'll start dinner. First, you need to work things out with Army." She glances sideways at Army, who has wandered into the garage. Why am I surprised that nothing gets past the detective I live with?

I join Army in the garage. "I'm sorry that I opened my mouth about the investigation before you're ready."

"No, I am sorry. I should not have talked to you that way. Please forgive me." He extends his hand to me.

I shake it. "Nothing to forgive, Army. We've been friends for too long."

"Gracias. Tomorrow we will begin again."

"About that, I'm going to score some points with Karen and help with the restoration of the hacienda for the next few days."

"Please, I do not want to make you feel that your help is unwanted," Army says. "I think I am putting pressure on myself to solve this."

I hesitate, then say, "I've…noticed that…umm…you have a…number of friends and family involved in the situation. Are you concerned you may be faced with a conflict of interest?"

Army looks at the ground and shrugs. "Yes, and it does not help. I need straight answers, but I have to face these people at family gatherings, too. Again, I did not mean to offend you."

"And I'm not offended in any way. I owe Karen a vacation. She's very excited to start working, and I'm sure I have enough skills to help with something. I've missed spending time with her. So, you continue the investigation, and just remember that I'll be here if you need me."

Army slaps me on the back. "If that is what you want. Now, let us enjoy our evening."

We join Eva and Karen in the kitchen. While we were gone, Sara had dropped off a chicken stew, along with rice, beans, and a loaf of crusty bread. Army brings a bottle of reposado tequila to the table, and soon he and I are drinking shots and reminiscing about cases we worked when we were young. Laughing like old friends do. Karen and Eva add their memories of living with us during those times as well.

We finish eating and are cleaning up when a knock at the door catches our attention. Eva jumps up and answers it. "I am glad you are here."

In walks a man roughly five-foot-ten, his black hair dusted with grey. Laying her hand on his arm, Eva announces, "This is a friend of mine, Marco. He's an art dealer and expert on 1800s Latin American art. I have asked him to help locate appropriate pieces for the hacienda."

We each introduce ourselves, and Marco joins us at the table.

"I'm excited to see what the place looks like," he says. "I've done some research, but actually being inside the hacienda will help me with scale and the number of pieces needed."

"How did you get started as an art dealer?" Karen asks.

"I started working at a gallery in Milwaukee, Wisconsin, for many years, but I grew tired of the winters there. I moved to Arizona, opened my own gallery, then found I was making multiple trips to Mexico to obtain works of art. I decided to try living and working here. I have a small gallery in Guadalajara, but the majority of my business is on the internet."

"That sounds wonderful," Karen interjects.

She and Eva spread out pictures of the hacienda's interior. Soon their conversation focuses on acquiring the major items needed and setting the budget. Marco is confident that he knows enough reputable dealers that he can find pieces at fair prices. Discussion continues around whether pieces can be reproductions or not. Army and I move to the living room with a bottle of tequila. Snippets of conversation are heard, each phrase filled with excitement and joy. Later, Marco leaves with a list of items and a plan to tour the hacienda for the precise measurements.

Karen and I head off to bed. "Marco seems nice," I say.

"He is, and he's smart. I think he'll be a great resource for the project. Pictures and books can only do so much," Karen replies. "I'm excited at how the project is starting. I think it's a good omen."

CHAPTER 9

The next morning, I awake early to the chirping of birds and what looks to be the start of a brilliant day. I turn my head toward Karen and see that she's awake, staring at the ceiling and moving her lips without speaking. I know she's working something out.

She rolls toward me and catches me staring. "What? Do I look that bad?"

"No, you're beautiful," I say. "I'm sorry, it's not you, I was just thinking about Army and our vacations that always get so complicated." I push myself up a little closer and kiss her cheek. "Everything is going to be okay. Trust me." I wink at her. She rolls her eyes at me, and I smirk. "Well, usually it turns out okay."

Karen laughs. "I'm glad you and Army are good again. I'd hate to see this investigation hurt your friendship *and* our vacation."

"Yeah, me too," I say. "But I think Army is still bugged about something. I'm not sure what. I wonder if he's got some history he's not telling me about."

"You sure you want to work on the hacienda today? I'd understand if you want to go with Army." I must have had a surprised look on my face. "I didn't say I'd like it, but I know you."

"I think I'll give Army some space for now, and besides, I think I'd like to spend a little time with you." I trace my finger down her arm and gently kiss her shoulder. "You know . . . working with Army has really cut into our time." I wiggle my eyebrows at Karen and push myself close enough to kiss her on the neck. "I know it's my fault, and I'd like to make it up to you."

"That would be nice." As she pulls me closer, I can feel her warmth as I breathe in the spicy aroma of her perfume. I close my eyes to soak it all in. "I miss you."

"I miss you too, but I'm also excited to see the project through. It would be great to have your help at the hacienda today." She hugs me tighter.

"I'll be happy to help any way I can."

"So, after breakfast, you'll talk to Army about what tools he has and pull together the ones you think we'll need?"

Snuggling into her, I snort a quiet laugh. "I can do that."

"And then you promise to help me *all* day, and not run off at the slightest murder?"

"I promise."

Karen kisses me on the ear. We snuggle for a few minutes, then her pragmatic side emerges. "We need to get moving. I'm going to take a shower."

"I'm going to just lay here for a minute." I'm sure she shoots me a look, but I don't care. I'm enjoying the moment.

A little later, I step out of the bedroom, heading for the shower. Karen and I finish getting ready and join Army and

Eva in the kitchen. At the table, Eva and Karen discuss projects they would like to work on at the hacienda, which gives me a better idea of what tools are necessary.

Army's standing at the counter while they talk, looking out the window. He nods toward the garage. "Dan, there's a toolbox in there. Look through it and grab anything else you might need."

Once we're at the hacienda, I'm assigned to start with demolition in the kitchen, as none of it is original. Eva and Karen plan to start on the fountain and garden area. The new roof is scheduled to be completed in a few days, and then interior work can begin. I happily pull out cabinets, displacing mice and other small creatures.

"Hello!" comes a singsongy voice from the courtyard.

Stepping out from the kitchen, I see a beautiful woman in her forties, about five feet, seven inches tall, with a short, fashionable haircut and dressed in a white pant suit that must have been custom fit, with matching open-toed wedge sandals. "Who are *you*?" she asks in English.

"Dan. Can I help you with something?"

"If only," she coos. I knit my eyebrows together. I'm not sure what she meant by that.

"Marcyellene? Why are you here?" Eva's voice comes from behind me. I turn to look, and her eyes are hard and cold. Karen stands a few feet behind her.

"Eva, dear, it is good to see you. I came to discuss a few ideas I've had since our last committee meeting. I think they will be wonderful additions to the project."

Anger flicks in Eva's eyes as she puts her hands on her

hips. "The committee has decided on the design elements for the project. I am not about to start making changes without the other committee members' consent."

"My concern is that Alejo is being allowed broad creative license, and I had several ideas that were dismissed. I would like to see them incorporated before this becomes a shrine to his father-in-law."

"The committee made the decisions as a group. I plan to uphold that trust. Alejo is *not* in charge," Eva snaps.

Marcyellene oozes false sympathy. "I am sorry. I do not want to cause any problems. Oh, I have been meaning to ask, is everything okay with Carlota? I have been very concerned."

Eva crosses her arms. "Everything is fine. Why are you concerned?"

"I have it on good authority that your delicious-looking brother-in-law, Victor, has stopped by a number of times in the last month. I am convinced that he is lending support for whatever is happening."

"We are family and always support each other. Who told you he was there?"

"It is not important. I am sure there is nothing to it." She grins at Eva.

A tight smile creases Eva's lips. "Marcyellene, are you staying to help?"

She scoffs. "Dressed like this? I wish I could, but I am off to a charity luncheon in Guadalajara. Speaking of clothes, no matter how many times I see you in that outfit, I love it because it is just so . . . *you*." She turns and waves over her shoulder as she walks to her car. "Ciao!"

Eva groans as she stomps her feet. "Ugh. That, that . . . woman. She can make my blood boil."

Karen wraps her arm around Eva's shoulders. "Who is she?"

Her name is Marcyellene Clara. She was born here but moved to the U.S. when she was a child, then at twenty years old married a Mexican man forty-five years her senior, who died rather *suddenly*." Her tone left no question as to her suspicions. "She got all his money, *and* the money of her second husband, who fell from a cliff while they were on vacation in Acapulco. The woman lives on a steady diet of gossip spreading and wooing other women's husbands." I feel myself blush at the thought that Marcyellene was flirting with me.

"She seems kinda catty, if you know what I mean," Karen says.

"She has a heightened sense of importance, and her money gets most of what she wants. She was so difficult to work with in the committee." Eva takes a deep breath. "I am sorry. Let us return to work and forget her."

After a few hours, Karen stops in to check on me. "Wow, this looks great. A clean slate."

"Thank you, and thank you. Are you ready to take a break?"

"Sure. I just had the most fascinating conversation with an elderly woman. I noticed her standing in the garden, and I guess she was curious and stopped in. She seems to know about this house."

"What did she say?"

"She introduced herself as María. She remembers the house from when she was a little girl. People coming and going for fancy parties."

"She must have some interesting stories. Anything else?"

"She certainly has opinions about the exterior paint color, and what we should do with the fountain. She was upset about the plastic roof that covers the center courtyard. Also, she said that the flowers in the courtyard need to be a mixture of yucca, dahlias, marigolds and sword lilies."

"I know the first three, but what's a sword lily?"

"Gladiolus, because of their shape," Karen replies. "I agree with using only native and period-correct plants, but we need to be careful of the message we send with which plants are chosen."

"Which plants are you worried about?"

"I was looking through the flower books, and plants like the sunflower, Mexican poppy, and gladiolus have been used to symbolize war and death."

"Sunflowers, really?" I ask incredulously.

"Yeah, as a matter of fact, it was the Aztec symbol of war. Maybe I'll come up with some suggestions and Eva and Sara can decide what they want to do." Karen wags her finger while she talks. "Just before she left, María said, 'The conquistador brings evil.' I think she was talking about the suit of armor that's in one of the bedrooms. I was going to show her that it's just a reproduction, but when I turned around, she was gone. It was spooky. She just seemed to disappear. And this makes two warnings about a conquistador since we've been here."

"She just left?"

"Yeah, but I hope she stops by again. I'd love to hear more about the house and show her our progress. Eva and I are headed to the market to talk to a couple of local artists about trying to recreate the metalwork and the wooden accents. Would you like to come?"

I don't have to think twice. "You bet!"

It's a perfect day. The sun is warm, but not too hot. A slight breeze brings the scents of spices, hot oil, and fresh bread as we pass neighborhood houses on the way to the market. Several people are outside sweeping their sidewalks in a futile attempt to keep the dirt at bay. They smile as we step through their work zone. Some mumble, "Buenas tardes." I fear our pilgrimage only serves to stir up the enemy they're fighting. I mumble, "Perdón," in return.

Approaching the eastern edge of town, voices can be heard, spices reach my nose, and then an explosion of color erupts in front of us. The market is a simple wooden pillar-and-post construction, with a slat roof and open sides. Vendor stalls circle the perimeter, and four are also grouped in the center.

Karen suddenly stops walking. "Wow. This is amazing! I don't know where to look first." Her eyes focus on a particular stand. "I see what I want. I'm heading for the dessert cart."

Eva breaks in. "First, we need to talk to Sebastian and Brad."

"I'm so sorry, Eva. You're right," Karen mumbles.

We visit a stall with intricate wooden carvings. Eva introduces us to Brad Carpenter. He's a head shorter than I am, with black, cropped hair, and he's probably in his late thirties. I extend my arm and shake a firm, calloused hand. "Nice to meet you, Brad."

"Nice to meet you, fellow American," he replies with a broad, white smile.

"Where are you from originally?"

Laughing, he says, "Minneapolis. I never fit into the corporate world, so I escaped. Woodworking is my passion, so I decided to try and make a living down here."

"Happy?" I question.

He nods. "Love it."

Eva pulls the drawings and pictures out of her bag when a young man appears from behind a curtain at the back of the stall. He's maybe twenty-one years old, has the same black hair as Brad, but is tall with a lean build. "This is my nephew, Lad," Brad introduces.

Lad waves. "Hey, Unc, you mind if I skip for a few? There's a sweet thing working at the piñata stall that I wanna check out."

Brad nods, then turns to us and shrugs his shoulders. He examines the pictures and drawings of the wooden accent. Eva asks, "Are you able to recreate these pieces with period-correct wood?"

He shakes his head. "I'd get a better feel for it if I could see the place."

Eva and Brad agree to meet at the hacienda in two days. Eva motions for us to move to Sebastian's stall, which is across from the bakery. Leaning into Karen, I whisper, "Looks like a win-win."

Karen nods. "So many sugary delights, so little time."

Eva introduces us to Sebastian, who is rail-thin with an even thinner mustache. His rat-like features are all sharp angles, with his narrow nose, black beady eyes, and nervous movements. He gives me an uneasy feeling, but I don't know why. The stall is filled with various metal works of art.

Trellises, cut-out silhouettes of animals, plants, the sun and the moon. Eva begins speaking to him in Spanish, and he seems less than excited about the job. During the conversation, he wags his finger, shrugs his shoulders, and looks at the ground, but after several minutes, he nods and shakes Eva's hand.

We move toward the dessert chart. Karen asks, "He didn't seem excited about the project. Why?"

"It is an ethical dilemma. The Preservation Society has come up against opposition before. People say it glorifies Spain's rule over México. But good or bad, that is part of *our* history. Sebastian will do the job because he cannot pass up paying work."

"Great, another step in the renovation resolved," Karen says.

Eva turns to us. "Let's pick up some desserts for after dinner tonight. Would you like to try tres leches cake and flan?" Eva orders four large slices of each, along with eight brightly decorated cookies. She brushes off my offer to pay.

We arrive home, and Sara and Victor are at the kitchen table with Army. Spanish switches to English. "Sara and Victor are staying for dinner." Army moves to the refrigerator and removes a wax paper package. "Nice to know someone in the beef business. I will grill these beautiful steaks."

Eva hands him a plate and tongs. "Dan and Victor, each of you grab a beer and supervise Army out there, please. We will pull everything together in here."

Outside, Army quickly has the grill heated up. While appearing to focus on the steaks, he says, "Victor, I know you have been using La Constancia Plantation for grazing and watering your cattle."

Victor's head snaps up in surprise. "We have gone so long without rain. Water is worth more than gold to me right now, and La Constancia has a deep well."

Army nods, sipping his beer and staring at the steaks. "I need you to stay away from there for the next few days."

"Why? Are you planning something?" I ask.

"More like I am working on a plan. I will know more soon."

"If you need me, just ask," I say.

Army bows his head. "Gracias, amigo. I have your promise, Victor?"

Victor nods his head, but invests little energy to it. Army is up to something. He always gets vague when he has an idea and is reluctant to involve others. How do I get him to understand that I still have his back no matter what?

CHAPTER 10

Army and Eva retire to their room. I'm lying in bed with Karen but can't fall asleep.

"What's the matter?" she asks.

"Nothing."

"Well, it's something, because you've turned over almost a dozen times, and every time you do, there's a bounce on the mattress and it wakes me up. So either lie still or get up, please."

"Sorry. You're right. I'm positive Army's planning something, but I can't get him to talk about it."

Karen rolls over and lays her hand on my shoulder. "Army will tell you when he's ready. Give him time."

"I know, but it still bugs me. I'm gonna get up and read for a while." I dress and head out to sit at the table. I'm not there long before Army steps out of his bedroom in his white uniform shirt and black pants. He doesn't see me until the last second. "Dios mío, you scared me sitting there so quiet. What are you doing up?"

"I could ask you the same question. Where are you going?"

"Just something I need to check on. Nothing important. Go back to bed. I will see you in the morning."

I'm put off some by being left out, but I don't let it deter me. "Give me a minute and I'll go with you."

"No, amigo. Just stay here." Army attaches his duty belt to his waist and steps toward the door.

"You know, the only thing more noticeable at night than a white shirt with brass stars on the collar would be if you wore a neon yellow vest. You're a smart guy, and this isn't smart. Let me help."

Army puts up his hand as if willing me to stop talking. "There is nothing to help with. I will see you at breakfast and tell you every boring thing then. Buenas noches." He closes the door behind him on his way out.

I'm torn between going after him and letting him do what he thinks is best. I decide to trust Army, but I don't like it. I take a book and move to the living room couch, planning to wait for him to come home. I can't seem to concentrate and alternate between pacing and attempting to read.

I must have fallen asleep on the couch because the next thing I know, the sound of the back door opening wakes me. The room is filled with early morning sunlight. I sit up and look into the kitchen. Army is seated at the table, his white shirt collar stained with blood and a wad of bandages pressed to his neck and right hand. His face is creased with fatigue.

I jump up and head over to him. "Holy cow, Army. What happened? Are you all right?"

He closes his eyes. "Shhhh, my friend. Don't wake Eva. It looks worse than it is."

"She's gonna figure it out sooner or later. What happened to you? I knew I should've been there."

Army pulls the bandages back from his neck. It looks as if the bleeding has stopped. There is a fine cut on the left side that extends from under his chin to his ear. "No, you did not need to be there. I had luck on my side."

"This is what you call luck? Were you attacked?"

"Sí. I was staking out La Constancia when someone came from behind me. They tried to garrote me, but part of the wire caught on a star on my right collar. I had enough time and room to get my hand between my neck and the wire. We were struggling, and then suddenly we were both knocked to the ground. Whoever it was let go of the wire. He was gone when I looked up."

"What knocked you to the ground?" I ask.

"Not what, but who. Ernesto. That amazing, wonderful goat came out of nowhere and head-butted my assailant. I had a first aid kit in the truck, so Jesús helped bandage me up and I came home."

My mind races with how bad this could have ended and that Army's backup wasn't his oldest partner, but a stupid goat.

"There's only one problem," Army says.

"Only one?" I ask. "I can think of a few more, but what's the one you're thinking of?"

"Ernesto is a terrible witness. He cannot give a description of the suspect." Army flashes his signature smile.

"Jesús was there too. Did he see your attacker? Or a vehicle? Anything?" My ire is rising.

"Yes, Jesús thinks that 'El Diablo' attacked me."

"The devil? Really? That's his explanation?"

"Well, El Diablo is a nice change from El Chupacabra."

Army laughs. I'm about to offer a smart-ass retort when I'm interrupted by Eva's gasp. "Dios mío, ¿Qué pasó?"

She rushes to Army's side, speaking Spanish too fast for me to fully understand. Eva's tone is more concern than anger. Army's demeanor is one of calm, downplaying the situation. I walk into the living room to give Eva and Army their privacy, but at the same time, I'm so angry I could punch a wall. At that moment, Karen emerges from the bedroom, still in her pajamas and robe. "What's going on?"

"Army was attacked last night."

"Attacked? Here in the house? I don't understand."

"He went on a stakeout last night without me. He could've been killed," I snap.

Karen shakes her head and holds up her index fingers. "Slow down. Is he all right? What happened?"

I go over the situation. "I should've been there. I should've insisted going along, and then none of this would've ever happened."

Karen crosses her arms over her chest. "Dan, you don't know that. More importantly, it could have been you. I love Army, but I love you more." Her eyes search mine. I'm at a loss for words, but she isn't. "This case is getting dangerous, and you seem to have forgotten that you're *not* a cop here. You're a civilian. I'm really scared for you, and this needs to stop!"

I drop my head to my chest and take a deep breath. "I'm sorry. You're right. However, you know I'll be fine. I'm like a cockroach," I say, trying to add some levity. "We survive everything from nuclear disasters to bad vacations."

Karen closes her eyes and sighs. "Part of what woke me up was that I had the weirdest dream. When I rolled over, you weren't in bed, so I came out to check on you."

"I'm fine. I think Army will be fine too. Do you remember your dream?"

"Yeah, I was at the hacienda, standing in the courtyard. It was at night with little light. I heard Army yelling for help but couldn't see him. I didn't know where you were, and I called your name and his over and over. My legs were so heavy that I couldn't move very fast. I noticed something, movement in one of the rooms. I was afraid."

"What was it?" I ask.

"I think it was another person."

"Who was it?"

Karen cocks her head to one side as if to draw up the scene. "I'm not sure. I couldn't see clearly, but someone started toward me. As they got closer, I had the feeling that I'd met them before, or I should've known who they were. I had the sense it was a bad man. I was frozen in place, and as his face got closer, I woke up." She rubs the palm of her hand on her forehead. "I was left with this feeling that I'll meet this guy again, but in real life, here."

I wrap Karen in my arms, kissing the top of her head. I wish I could make everything all right. I'm torn between giving Karen the vacation she deserves and helping my best friend solve these crimes. This is bad.

Army and Eva enter the room, holding hands. Army rubs his forehead. "I am sorry, amigos. This is not the visit I wanted for you. I do need to do some follow-up at the scene, but I promise

voice serious, "I will stay and help if you want. Nothing is more important to me than you."

Karen kisses me on the cheek. "I know, but I'm fine. The sun is shining. No evil shadows. Eva is here with me. If I need anything, you're a phone call away. You and Army need to get this done."

I walk as far as the courtyard; Karen having nightmares has me on edge. I can't help but feel that my time and attention would be better served staying close to her. Lost in thought, Karen's voice snaps me back to the present. "Dan!"

"What?"

"Army is waiting in the truck. You need to go."

Another hug and kiss for Karen. "Until tonight," I say, wiggling my eyebrows.

"Ugh, go!" Karen slaps my arm with a laugh, turns, and heads back inside.

Once in the truck, we head to La Constancia Plantation. Army pulls into the driveway, then stops. "We will walk in. I do not want to risk driving over any possible evidence." I nod in agreement. We head to the back of the Blazer. Army grabs the camera, and I get the evidence kit. We both put on gloves and do what we've been doing for years.

"*This* time, all the evidence will be locked in the evidence locker at the station," Army says.

"You don't want to take the chance of someone breaking into the house this time, huh?"

"No, my friend, I have as you say, 'a learning curve.'"

We each take a side of the driveway and slowly walk in, surveying for items that are out of place, even the garbage.

Food wrappers, cigarette butts, cups, napkins are all tagged, photographed, and put into numbered evidence bags. No idea what could have been left by the thieves and somehow made its way there. About a hundred yards in, Army heads up a small incline and stops at an overgrown bush. "This is where I was staked out when I was attacked."

Dried blood drops sit in the dirt. I scrape up the dirt and place it in a paper envelope. "I ended up at the bottom here after the suspect and I tumbled down the hill," Army points.

"There are a number of hoofprints and a boot print in this pile of mud, and before you say anything, I know it's not mud, but I'm gonna pretend it is if I'm the one taking the plaster mold."

"Okay, Dan, it is animal mud." He laughs, shaking his head. I head back to the truck for the plaster and bucket, mix it with water, and pour it into the print. While it sets, we continue to find and label evidence. When the plaster hardens, I pull it back and inspect the impression. "It appears to be the right boot. Whoever it belongs to is missing the right corner of that heel. Now all we have to do is find the owner."

"Sí, but in cattle country, it is not a narrow field."

"Let's hope we get lucky, then."

Half of the garrote is found at the bottom of the hill, dislodged in the struggle. Braided wire looped around a wooden dowel. Homemade weapon, silent, easily concealed, and deadly. The victim wouldn't have much reaction time, and there would be no sound to draw attention.

Army's voice brings me out of my thoughts. "I think we have learned everything this place has to offer. The ground is dry and hard, so I do not see any usable tire tracks. I think it is time to head back to the station and catalogue the evidence."

"Sounds like a plan."

At the station, we log in the evidence, download the photos, and make sure it's all locked up before heading over to the hacienda.

We meet Karen and Eva at home to shower and change for our night out. Walking to the town square on this perfect night, I begin to relax. The sun is down, and the air is slightly cool. As we approach, I hear music playing and smell hot oil and spices in the air. My stomach growls.

The square is energized. Colored lights, a three-piece band on a small wooden stage, food and merchandise vendors lining both sides of the street. I grab Karen's hand and twirl her around. She does the same to me. Laughing and swaying, we make our way down the street.

"Let us get something to eat. We missed lunch today," Army says, walking straight to a taco stand. Karen and Eva look for an open table while Army and I order a variety of soft tacos. After dropping off the plates, I look for beverages, tequila for Army and me and wine for Karen and Eva. We sit listening to the music, eating, talking, and laughing.

"Dan, I would like dessert. Would you be a dear and pick something out, please?" Karen asks.

"Yes, love of my life, I will." I make my way to the stall that's serving desserts. There're six people ahead of me, so waiting in line gives me time to look around. The street is crowded. Everyone from town must be here. My eyes wander around the area near me, the broken asphalt road with no curbs.

It melts into grass, or really just dirt, on the side of the road. A plastic cup lies on its side, its contents spilled, never to be savored. *How sad. I hope it wasn't a glass of tequila.'* But then I notice that a boot heel made an impression in the wet dirt. The right corner of the right heel is missing. Army's attacker is here!

I abandon my place in line and try to follow what I suspect would be the person's trajectory. I have my head down looking for any additional heel prints when I bump into someone.

"Oh, excuse me," I say, then look up. It's Emilio Mendoza.

"Walking around with your head down is a good way to get . . . hurt," Emilio replies.

This guy just gets under my skin, from being rude to Army, to stealing from people in the village, to having no empathy for his brother's loss. Making eye contact, I force a smile. "No worries. Everyone here is so *friendly.*"

"Really? That is not what I heard. Your friend found out the hard way. Take my advice, keep your head up and out of matters that do not concern you!" He and his polished dress shoes turn and walk away. Damn, I'd love for him to be Army's attacker and watch him be arrested. Asshole! Wait, how does he know about Army being attacked?

"Dan!" Karen's voice snaps me back to reality. "Did you forget about the desserts?"

"Ahhhhh, no. Just thought I saw something better over here."

"Here . . . at the piñata stand?"

"Sorry, it looked like something else from a distance. I'll get the desserts now."

Once the desserts are purchased and eaten, Karen and Eva

head off to get another glass of wine. We're alone, so I explain to Army what I saw and my conversation with Emilio.

"I am not surprised by anything he says," Army states.

"Too bad he's not the guy we're looking for. I'd pay money to see him in shackles."

"His time will come. I am convinced."

"Would it be weird to ask everyone here to show us their boots in hopes of finding your attacker?"

"Sí, that would be extraño. For now, no more police work. Let us dance with our wives, drink more tequila, and enjoy the night." I'm not happy that Army appears to take everything in stride, but for this moment, I try to live with it.

CHAPTER 11

We enjoy our evening until the band stops playing. "I think it is time to head home, amigos," Eva says. "Karen and I have much to do at the hacienda tomorrow."

"I'm excited. Every day the place comes together more and more," Karen adds. "I just wish Alejo would stop showing up. He acts like he's the project manager."

"Is he a problem?" I ask.

"No, he is an ass!" Our heads collectively snap over to look at Eva. We rarely hear negative comments from her. "What? He is," she replies. "Always going on about how much he knows and what would be best. 'Ohhh, the glory of Spain.' Estúpido!" I'm so caught off guard, I can't think of anything to say. Army just shakes his head.

Karen laughs. "Maybe we should suggest Alejo take a trip to Spain as our in-depth researcher on traditional Spanish haciendas for weeks . . . I mean months, at his own expense, of course."

"I like how you think, chica," Eva says. I believe that Eva is joining Team Karen on how to be devious.

"Eva, be kind. Alejo did pay for a whole new roof, and that could not have been cheap," Army says.

Eva turns slowly, her eyes narrow and fixated on Army. I feel for Army as I know that look from Karen, and it never ends well for me. "Yes, he did, but it would have been less painful to have the Preservation Society pay for it than listen to him tell us over and over again that he did it."

Army averts his gaze and says nothing. I deftly change subjects. "Hey, guys, thanks for a wonderful evening. This was fun."

Army's shoulders relax, and he sighs, pressing a smile to his lips. "I am glad you enjoyed yourselves. It is our pleasure to show our guests a good time."

We walk along in silence the rest of the way home. Once there, we say our good nights and head off to bed. I sleep wonderfully.

The next morning, I wake early and shower and get dressed before anyone else is up. Still thinking about the attack on Army, I decide to take a walk around town. There is no one else on the street. The air is cool and damp. It must have rained during the night, just enough to wet everything down but not enough to make a dent in the drought-like conditions. I slowly walk to the main street, past shop windows, and check out their wares. I feel bad for the area. Everything is drying up and turning to dust. I know everyone wishes it would start to rain. This town needs a true benefactor that can bring jobs, money, and well-being.

I see a cemetery across an open field and decide to explore. My shoes are damp by the time I reach the churchyard. The headstones are old with intricately carved headstones. Some tilt to one side or the other, covered in moss. It hurts to see the graves of children and wonder what happened. The town's history is preserved here. I see the name 'Gómez' engraved on several markers. I'll have to ask Army if he has family buried here. One has his name, and I wonder if he was named for a relative. Slowly, I make my way around and between the stones, then finish my self-guided tour of the cemetery. Wandering nowhere in particular, I cut across a field on the other side and head for the edge of town. My tennis shoes are at risk given the piles of animal manure. Cow, horse, sheep, or goat, I can't tell. My attention is suddenly caught by a print of a boot missing the right corner on the right heel. The suspect's print, side by side with goat tracks!

I follow the trail. The two sets of prints appear to be side by side. My mind is racing. Jesús and Ernesto? Is all Jesús' talk about the Chupacabra just elaborate deception and he's behind Juan Mercado's death? But why? What good would it do to kill him? Is Jesús a fanatic hoping to keep the area undeveloped?

Soon the tracks seem to separate. I'm torn between following the boot print as far as possible, but I don't want to walk too far. I race back to the house, hoping against hope that the evidence isn't lost before I can get back with Army. I retrace my steps, taking a more direct route back than I did to get here. The town is waking up. Cars are on the roads, people are walking on the sidewalks, and kids are playing in a nearby lot. I nod and say "¡Buenos días!" to those who make eye contact as I move faster than my knees like.

I burst through the back door with such force that everyone at the kitchen table jumps. Karen spills her coffee. "Dan! What's the matter with you?"

I rush into my explanation of my walk, the heel prints, goat tracks, and my theory that Jesús may be the killer.

Army breaks in, "Amigo, breathe! Sit down and start over, slowly." Eva hands me a cup of coffee, and I again describe what I found and where.

"I will go and investigate, but I find it hard to believe that Jesús is our killer," Army says flatly, shaking his head.

I'm taken aback. "Army, you know better than to make up your mind about a case before all the evidence is in. The evidence leads an investigation."

His voice is slow and deliberate. "I live here. I know these people, not you, and I'm not ignoring anything at this point. I'm making an observation based on *my* experience as chief of this town."

I guess I've been put in my place. I need to take a beat between what my mind thinks and what I say. I don't want to alienate Army, but rather find whoever did this. "Okay . . . whenever you're ready, we can go."

"No, Dan, you take a day off. I want Diego to get more experience with investigations and the handling of evidence," Army replies.

I guess I'm being shut out from the case *AGAIN,* but why? I make eye contact with him. Do I see anger or fear? I step away from the table and head into our bedroom before I say something I'll regret. Karen joins me. I shut the door and spin around to face her. "This is crap!"

"What do you think is going on here?" she asks softly.

"Army's not letting me help with the investigation. He knows something, but I don't know what. I think he's making sure that family isn't involved."

"Why would Army do that? Who would it benefit?"

"Him! He does live here. Maybe he's being pressured by someone."

Karen sighs, dropping her shoulders. "Do you trust Army, as your best friend, to do an honest job?"

"Yes. Maybe." I rub my forehead. "I don't know."

"Then let him do his thing in his own way. Be available and supportive. When he's ready, he'll tell you what he's up to and why." She kisses my cheek and whispers in my ear, "For now, you can be my hacienda slave and spend the day with me!"

"Fine, but I don't have to like what Army's doing."

"You're right. You don't have to like it. Just give him time. I'll make you a slave with some exclusive 'benefits'," she says with a wink.

I know what she means and relax some. "I'd love to do your bidding." Taking a deep breath, I decide to be like the tortoise, slow and steady, not rushing to judgment.

I hear the back door close. Through the windows, I see the Trailblazer pull into the street and drive in the direction of the field I mentioned. Karen sees me staring out the window. "Dan, let it go. I want us to have a nice day together."

"I'm sorry. You're right. We'll have a good time. It'll be fun," I say, trying to add some positive energy to my words.

Karen and I leave the bedroom, where Eva is waiting with several paint cans and supplies. I grab as much as I can carry while Eva opens the door, and the three of us step out onto the sidewalk. The day is starting to warm up. Everything is drying out again. A short walk, and we arrive at the hacienda. Eva stops suddenly and looks at the front door. It's slightly ajar.

"I know I locked that last night. Sara and I should be the only ones with keys now."

I put down the cans of paint. "Stay here." I push the door open the rest of the way and peek in. Creeping along the wall, I scan the courtyard. I hear a noise, as if someone is moving things in the direction of the living room. I quickly move to the door, waiting for my eyes to adjust to the dimly lit room. I notice the figure of a man with his back to me. He's about my height and appears to be assembling something.

"Can I help you with something?" I ask.

He jumps and spins around. "No. I just wanted to get an early start today."

"Alejo?" Eva asks, having followed me in. "What are you doing, and how did you get in?"

Alejo waves his hand as if to dismiss her questions. "The former key holder gave me an extra key, as he was aware of my need to have unlimited access on my project."

"This is not *YOUR* project," Eva snaps. "It is the Preservation Society's. You need to give me that key, right now." She holds out her hand.

Alejo makes no attempt to retrieve his key. "I have been a very generous benefactor and feel I deserve more than a little latitude on overseeing the process."

Karen coos softly, playing to Alejo's ego. "And we thank you for everything. We're more than grateful for the support you've provided. However, the Society does have expectations. The Board of Directors have tasked Eva and Sara to be responsible for what happens on-site. I know that Eva, Sara, and I would feel terrible if something happened to you while you were here alone, so from now on, please ask Eva or Sara to let you in. May I have your key, please?"

Alejo hesitates, then reluctantly pulls the key from his pocket and hands it to Karen.

"Thank you. Oh, what have you brought us? It looks wonderful," Karen says.

"It is an authentic Spanish matador's costume. My father-in-law's father was one of the finest bullfighters in all of Spain, and I thought it would make a worthy addition to the collection. I feel it deserves to be displayed in the living room, given its historical significance."

"Then we will have to try not to splatter on it while we are painting today," Eva states with more than a hint of sarcasm. She puts her hands on her hips.

"If you people are painting, then I will need to take this back with me. It is too precious to risk damage to it," Alejo replies.

"If you think that's best," Karen says. "You're welcome to stay and help us paint. We could use your support."

Alejo picks up the costume and walks to the door, calling over his shoulder, "I don't paint."

"Elvis has left the building," I say.

"I have said it once, and I will say it again. Asshole!" Eva calls after Alejo. We all laugh. "I can't believe you were so nice to him," she continues.

"I wanted the key from him and did what I needed to in order to get it," Karen replies.

Muttering under my breath, I note, "Like the spider to the fly."

"What was that, Dan?" Karen asks with a smirk on her face.

"Nothing. Nothing at all."

We tape the woodwork, cover the floors, and paint the living room for several hours with Eva's radio playing in the background. The Spanish music, being active, the warm tangerine color on the walls, and seeing the results of a morning's work all help to lighten my mood. Suddenly it's noon, and I realize I'm starving.

"I'd like to buy you ladies lunch, if I may."

"Gracias, Dan," says Eva. "I will walk with you to the market on the edge of town. I need to speak to several of the artists there about different commissions for the hacienda. Many vendors will be selling food, so you and Karen can have lunch and then walk back when you are done. I will get something later."

Paint cans sealed and brushes wrapped in plastic to stay moist, we head out. The noon sun is warm, but not hot. Walking down the broken sidewalk, holding Karen's hand on this beautiful Mexican day, I realize that this is the important stuff. The time I spend with my wife and friends, not being a detective. I need to work on my relationship with my friend Army, not my crime-solving partner Army. My competitive side can and has impacted relationships. I don't need to solve this case. He does. Social Worker Karen would call this 'positive self-talk.'

"Why are you smiling?" Karen asks me.

"Because I'm where I'm supposed to be, and I'm happy. Thank you for everything."

Her eyes fill with tears. I know that my being happy while

not being a cop anymore is important to her. "My resolution is to spend more time as a husband and friend than a cop." I can't resist adding, "Of course, being your slave tonight would make me even happier." I wiggle my eyebrows.

"Ugh, you're hopeless," she remarks, sniffling.

At the market, all my senses are engaged. Spices hit my nose, brightly colored clothes and piñatas hang everywhere, conversations and laughter carry through the air, desserts beg to be eaten, and soft woven blankets draw me to touch them. This is a place of joy, and I want us to be a part of it.

Eva points to several stalls. "They sell food. You could have lunch here, and I'll see you back at the hacienda."

Karen buys two cans of diet soda from a kiosk cart and finds a table while I order the tamales with rice and beans. She takes the chicken, and I take the beef. I open the corn husk skin on the tamale, letting the steam rise. Looking up, I see Emilio and Juan near a table of printed tee shirts. What are they doing here? I'm sure it's not shopping.

Emilio moves in very close to Juan's face and jabs his shoulder as he talks. Juan's head hangs down, and he slowly shakes it from side to side. Emilio's face is so red he could pop a blood vessel at any moment. Suddenly, Victor appears and physically moves both men through a door at the back of the stall.

"What would Victor be doing with Emilio and Juan?" I ask, looking at Karen.

Karen places her knife and fork on her plate. "And we have a new land speed record," she says with a sigh.

"Huh?"

"For the broken resolution of being more of a husband and less of a cop. What was it . . . fifteen minutes?"

"Oh. Sorry about that. It's an odd pairing, don't you think?"

"It's a small town. I'm sure many people end up doing business with people they don't like or wouldn't normally associate with because there's no one else."

"You could be right, but I'd still like to know what Emilio was so angry about," I say. "Juan just stood there."

"Can we please finish lunch before continuing the investigation?" Karen asks.

"Yes. You're right, I should just stop looking for suspects and motives."

"Well, it may be worth mentioning to Army, in case it's relative to the case," she says. "What am I saying? I'm a police detective enabler. This is all your fault." She shakes her finger at me.

"Wow. That's kinda funny. Let me make it up to you. What would you like for dessert?"

"Some of the ice cream, please."

"Sí, milady." As I head over to the dessert vendor, Victor reemerges through the door at the back of the tee shirts stall, but before he can close it, Emilio calls out something in Spanish, something that I translate into, "Tomorrow night, or everyone will know about something at the city end," or maybe he means the edge of town. Victor slams the door and continues walking. He doesn't seem to notice me, but he looks angry enough to kill. If I translated it correctly, maybe he already has. Juan Mercado's body was found in a field 'on the edge of town,' and Army was attacked at La Constancia located 'on the edge of town.' Is Victor our murderer? Army isn't going to want to hear that I suspect his brother-in-law.

"Are you waiting for them to make the ice cream?" Snapping back to reality, I realize Karen is standing next to me.

"Uh…no. Sorry, got a little distracted. Please help me, and pick out anything you would like."

"Okay. Let's also get some for a snack later this afternoon. We still have a few hours of painting left to do."

Karen points to the flavor she wants, and I pay. I turn around and bump into Emilio, who spits, "¡Vámos, estúpido!" He walks on, and Juan shuffles behind him. Head down, no eye contact, he has the appearance of a man whose spirit has been broken.

I feel bad for Juan. He loses his wife and has to deal with his jerk of a brother. I loathe Emilio. I hope Army finds evidence to convict him of some crime, any crime.

Karen is walking toward the sidewalk, waving me over. "Dan, we need to go."

"Coming, master," I mutter under my breath.

A slow walk back to the hacienda allows my mind to drift back to Emilio, Juan, and Victor, as what? Business partners? Rivals? Blackmailer/victim? Boss and employee? This situation gets curiouser and curiouser.

CHAPTER 12

Several hours later, paint has transformed the walls of the living room. The satisfaction of doing the job well and the beat of the music lift my mood. Karen passes by, and I grab her hand to dance. Swaying back and forth to the rhythm, we both laugh. I twirl her around, and Eva claps. "I see salsa dancing in your future."

"Not with my bad knees, but I'm enjoying myself right now," I say, giving Karen a hug and kiss before releasing her.

Karen squeezes my arm, laughing.

Looking around the room, I state, "This is starting to come together. I don't like to paint, but I love the results a coat of new color gives a room. If you need me to do any research on furniture or other items, just let me know."

Eva's eyes dance as she replies, "Thank you for the offer, but I have Marco working on that."

Army arrives to check on us. "¡Hola, amigos! ¿Cómo están?"

"Muy bien, ¿y tú?" I reply, remembering that above all else, this is my friend. I need to relax and enjoy this time together. Although I want to put myself back in the investigation, I bite my tongue to avoid asking if anything of interest was found after my tip in the field.

Walking through the place, he remarks, "This is beautiful, my friends. Good work. Maybe I will rent this team out as Hacienda Renovators, LLC."

"Mi esposo, I do not think you could afford to hire this level of talent. We are very expensive and exclusive." Eva kisses Army's cheek.

He asks, "Are we ready to head home for dinner?"

"I know I am," I reply.

We clean up our supplies, wrap the brushes in plastic wrap, and make sure the seals on the paint cans are tight. Brad will come by the house later with an update on the cabinets. I can start to picture the plan that was so abstract to me just a few days ago.

Once home, Army pulls me aside. "Thank you for understanding about today. I had Diego take the lead and explain to me what he would do next in the investigation. Someday I will retire, and the next generation of officers need to be trained."

"And? What did he do?" I ask hesitantly.

"We located the tracks near the cemetery. The hoofprint and the heel print were lost once they reached the concrete sidewalk. Diego decided he would follow up with Jesús regarding the heel marks since a goat's print was also there." Army shakes his head and laughs out loud. "It was a mess. But Jesús gave us permission to search the premises."

"Did Diego find the boot with the corner of the heel missing?"

"No," Army snickers, "but he did spend two hours going through every pair of shoes that Jesús owns. Apparently, he never throws anything out. No matter their condition. Thank goodness we wear gloves."

Frowning, I say, "Did Diego think to check the pair of boots Jesús was wearing?"

"*That* I had to remind him to do. So, good or bad, Jesús' boots did not match our print." He shrugs.

I'm not sure if I'm relieved or disappointed that for now Jesús has been eliminated. I remind myself that we still have a large pool of suspects left. Rubbing my forehead, I say, "Can you think of any way to narrow down who may own the boots we're looking for?"

Army silently shakes his head.

"I hate to say it, but I don't think they belong to Emilio. I've always seen him in dress shoes."

"Sí, he sees himself as a mover and shaker." Army crosses his arms across his chest. "But when he was younger, he helped move cattle for my dad."

"And ended up betraying him. What a turd," I spit out. "But that has me thinking he could have a pair of boots."

"You mean a pair that he occasionally wears. It is possible. I do not have enough evidence to request a search warrant, and I *know* he will not give me permission to search his house," Army replies. "Do not worry yourself. I am on it." He slaps me on the back, and I bite my tongue. Army is making it clear that I'm not investigating this.

Eva breaks in, "If you are discussing police work, could you stop for now? I would like us to have a relaxed evening."

Army bows his head, places his right hand over his heart, and smiles. "Sí, mi amor."

"Gracias, querido esposo," Eva replies with a smile, gently touching Army's chin.

Army, Eva, and I join Karen at the table. "Sara dropped off dinner for us while we were out," Eva states.

"This looks delicious," Karen says.

I take the first bite, and it's amazing. The tender meat has the perfect amount of spicy heat. "What is this? It's great."

Eva smiles, and her deep brown eyes dance with satisfaction. "Thank you. I am glad you like it. I was concerned because it can be a bit spicy. It is called birria."

"What's in it?" Karen asks.

"Different chilies, spices, onion, and normally goat meat," Eva replies.

I stop with a forkful of meat halfway to my mouth and think of Ernesto. My appetite wanes some.

"But Sara used beef." Eva giggles as she reads my face. A sigh of relief escapes me as I pop the meat in my mouth and snicker. We enjoy our food in relative silence as long-time friends can.

Looking up from her plate, Eva asks, "I think it will be a beautiful night for a walk if you are interested, Karen, Dan?"

Karen nods enthusiastically. "That sounds like a great idea. I'd love to explore more of the town. Thank you."

"Army is a great town historian," Eva adds. "His family has lived here for many generations."

"I was wondering about that. Walking through the cemetery, I noticed several headstones with the name Gómez on them." My spoon makes a scraping sound against my plate as I finish my rice and beans. "I meant to ask you, but completely forgot when I found the boot print." Eva passes the bowl of birria as well as more rice and beans.

"Sí, my family has been here a long time. My great-great-grandfather was once the mayor. I would love to show you more of my town," Army says with a smile.

Dinner finished, food put away, and kitchen cleaned up, we step out into the evening air. It's warm and moist, with the smell of rain approaching, that is, if hoping makes it true. Twilight has begun with a rosy sky above. Some of the neighboring homes have lights on, throwing eerie shadows onto the ground.

Army walks to the west as the three of us follow, much the same path I had taken earlier in the day. Arriving at the cemetery, Army points to a large, black, granite headstone tilting precariously backwards with the name "Gómez" boldly engraved in the center.

"That is my great-great-grandfather's headstone. It was a gift from the people of the town. He served for three terms." Pride saturates Army's voice. "Next to him are my mother's and father's graves. My father, too, was a great man. No matter how old I get, I miss them both every day." Army continues to point out headstones of family: aunts, uncles, and cousins. We then make our way out of the cemetery and onto the sidewalk, walking further west.

Sweeping his arm to both sides of the street, Army stops and says, "These row houses were built for the workers of the local sugar mill. When it was fully staffed, it employed over one hundred people."

Although painted in a variety of colors, many need serious repairs. One has its roof caved in, windows broken, no door, and charred remains for walls. "What happened to this one?" Karen looks to Army, pointing to it.

"That is a local mystery," Army replies. "It was before I moved back. A husband and wife were killed, and the house was set on fire."

Karen gasps. "How terrible. What happened?"

Army looks around as if making sure no one else is listening. "Rumor has it the couple was muling drugs for the cartel, got greedy, and cut themselves in on the money. The cartel made an example of them. However, none of this was ever proven, and no one was charged."

"That's horrible," Karen states.

"It was repaired once and suspiciously burned down again. No one has been willing to repair the place since. If you talk to some of our older people, they feel the space is cursed." Army shrugs and begins walking again. Further west, I see the outline of several abandoned buildings.

"What's that?" I ask, walking further down the street to get a better look.

"That is the old sugar mill. A new one was built about thirty years ago, on the other side of town. This is the land that Emilio owns and wanted as the site for the water park." Emilio, the water park location, Juan Mercado's death, and Army's family all seem to be swirling around in my head, but why?

There are eight abandoned buildings. The main one is a single-story, L-shaped red brick approximately the length of a football field. Its side closest to the road has collapsed and looks like a set of stairs. Bricks lay in various states of deterioration on the ground. Smaller sheds and silos surround the main one, and trees grow alongside and through most of the structures. This place has been long forgotten.

Karen turns to Eva. "Those bricks look like a good match to our courtyard pavers. Also, the ceiling looks to be wooden planks. Brad may be able to convert those into . . . I don't know, something cool."

Eva's eyes light up. "That would be my hope, too."

"Oh, we should look for any old furniture that could be restored, like tables."

"Do you think that Emilio might give us permission to look through the buildings for things that we could use at the hacienda?"

"That is a wonderful idea. Maybe tomorrow we can look around the buildings before I call him," Eva says with a sly grin on her face.

Army clicks his tongue. "Eva, that is trespassing."

"Well, who is listening to me? My husband or the Comisario General?" She turns her brown eyes on Army.

Army stops and faces her. "We are one in the same. I cannot separate them, and please do not ask me to."

Eva reluctantly nods. "You are right. I was wrong to ask. I will call Emilio when we get back home."

Army shakes his head. "Do not get your hopes up. I find it hard to believe that Emilio will give anything away."

"I will *still* ask," Eva says in a metered voice, as she is now the one who looks directly at Army. Army nods in deference.

"Did anyone bring a flashlight?" I ask, changing the subject. "If not, we may want to head back. It's getting dark."

Everyone agrees, and we start a slow walk home. Karen and Eva happily chat about possible finds at the old sugar mill and appear energized by the ideas. Army and I look at each other, roll our eyes, and smile.

Once back home, Eva contacts Emilio. "He has agreed to have someone meet us at the mill at 9:00 a.m. I called Sara and Brad to see if they would like to accompany us." Karen nods in agreement. "If Sara finds someone to watch the store, then she will try, but we should not wait for her. Brad will meet us there. Afterward, he would like us to go to his store to see the cabinets. He will not come here tonight, then."

Army and I make plans to check a few meat processing plants in the area tomorrow. He is hoping to find the trailer used in the cattle rustling, or any of the rustled cattle. We settle in to watch television before turning in for the night.

CHAPTER 13

Wandering into the kitchen this morning, I find Eva and Karen at the table with cups of coffee, strategizing their walk through the old mill. They have a list of specific items they hope to find, along with any building materials that Brad Carpenter may be able to use in recreating the wooden accent pieces. I help myself to coffee and sit next to Karen, who says, "¡Buenos días, mi amor!"

"¡Buenos días!" I reply, raising my cup. Eva starts making scrambled eggs and has tortillas warming in the oven. I help Karen pull other food out of the refrigerator. Army joins us, showered and casually dressed. After breakfast is finished, Eva and Karen leave for the mill.

"Amigo, can I ask for your help today?"

I purse my lips and take a breath. "Are you sure you want me with you?" I ask skeptically.

"Please?"

I nod in agreement.

"Okay. There are several cattle processing plants I would like to check out," Army states. "If we are lucky, we will find the cattle rustler's trailer."

Army and I spend hours checking out the cattle processing

plants. Some are little more than a shed surrounded by pens, which appear to be all but abandoned. No fresh blood or animal remains. I'm frustrated. Where are all the stolen cattle going?

We sit silently in the truck. I wait to hear what Army wants to do next.

He drums his fingers on the Trailblazer's steering wheel. "This appears to be, as you say, 'a wild geese chase.'"

"Goose," I say.

"What?"

"The expression is 'a wild goose chase,' not 'a wild geese chase.'"

Army shakes his head. "Either way. Geese or goose. It has been a waste of time. I am trying to remember a plant my father took me to many years ago." He pulls out his phone and searches for it. "Ah. I found it. It is a ninety-minute drive."

When we arrive at the Smith Processing Plant, Army finds a place to park. It's much larger than the other places we have visited. Cattle trailers line the outer fence. Men stand outside the pens in small groups, murmuring in Spanish. Some make eye contact, others don't but walk away. That type of movement gets my coppy senses going, but for now, I'll follow Army's lead.

Pointing to the sign, I comment, "Smith. Original name."

Army rolls his eyes. We start examining the tires of vehicles parked there, then look at the brands on the cows. The sound of a truck starting up catches our attention. Both of us head toward where it's pulling out when four men block our path. Three trailers are pulling toward the exit, and two pull in.

"¿En qué le puedo ayudar?" says one of the men with a smirk. He's about thirty-five years old, as round as he is tall, with slicked back, black hair. The other three men look like former linebackers for an American professional football team. None of them have the slightest hint of a smile.

Army moves forward while showing his badge. "¡Buenos días! Soy Comisario General Armando Gómez. ¿Cómo está?" Two of the linebackers take a step toward Army.

"Soy dueño de esta empresa. ¿Qué hace aquí?"

Army's face is serious. He switches to English, I'm sure for my benefit. "We are investigating a crime that involved the use of a trailer. We stopped on the chance that the trailer may also transport cattle."

The man looks between Army and me, then stares back at Army. "Comisario, I am sure that none of the drivers here would be involved in anything illegal. You wasted the trip." The man replies with arrogance, which makes me want to slap him.

Army smiles back, but his eyes remain serious. "You may be right, but do we have your permission to look around?"

"I am sorry. Today is very busy. Trucks are coming and going. It could be unsafe to have you walking around. I will need to ask you and your friend to leave because it is upsetting business. ¡Adiós!"

Army nods in acknowledgement. We start for the Trailblazer when he stops and turns back. "Would you know the driver that just left or what company he works for?"

The man replies nonchalantly, "I do not know which trailer you mean, and drivers, so many. I cannot remember them all."

We have been dismissed. As we near the Blazer, we find

that we've been parked in by several trailer trucks. Army calls out and points, "Have someone move these, so we can leave."

The man looks around and sarcastically replies, "I am not sure who they belong to. Please wait while I try to find out. Gracias."

Army and I climb into the Trailblazer, then sit and wait.

"Notice how he never gave us his name, and now he's making sure we can't follow that trailer," I state.

Army drums his fingers again. "I know, but why? He doesn't know if that is even the trailer we are looking for. All I could see was that the truck had a white cab and red lettering on the side. Did you see what it said?"

"Sorry, no. It was too far away, and a fence was blocking my view."

Almost twenty minutes later, one of the trailers moves, allowing us to pull out.

"We have no chance of finding which direction the trailer went," I say. Army bangs his fist on the steering wheel, then sits back and closes his eyes. When he reopens them, he rubs his chin and states, "Let's go home. There is nothing more we can do today. We will surprise our wives."

I'm sitting on the couch reading a book when Karen and Eva come in through the back door. "How did it go at the old mill?" I ask, looking up.

Karen's eyes light up. "It was great. Brad has some wonderful ideas for several things we found. I took pictures, and Eva tagged the items with duct tape. Then we spent time at the hacienda to double-check if the items will work. We also saw the cabinets Brad built. They're gorgeous."

"We hope to go back because we did not get through all the buildings today," Eva interjects. "Where is Armando?"

Laughing, I reply, "We both smelled like cow when we got home. I took a shower already, now it's Army's turn."

Eva nods and heads for the kitchen. Karen sits next to me and gives me a kiss. "I missed you today. I know we're helping Army, but I wish there was more us time."

"I know. Me, too." I kiss the top of her head. "What did Emilio say about the items you're interested in?"

"I took a ton of pictures at the mill. Emilio wasn't there, but one of his staff showed us around and told us about a restored hacienda in another town. The guy thought it was about a hundred miles away. We're thinking of taking a day to drive there and get some additional ideas before we work out a price with Emilio. Eva's trying to find out who she needs to talk to about getting inside and when."

Smiling, I reply, "Sounds like you had a better day than we did." I give her a condensed version of what happened.

"I'm sorry it didn't work out the way you wanted, but I'm glad you're home." Karen kisses me again, the kind of kiss that makes me want more, but she dances off toward the printer to download the pictures. I'm just so happy when she's happy. I am ready for a quiet evening at home.

Karen and Eva sort through the pictures, labeling possible design placements. Later, we settle in with a board game to end the evening before calling it a night. Sleeps comes easily for me.

"Dan . . . . . . *DAN*."

I jump out of bed onto my feet. "What?"

Dressed in his Chief's uniform, Army is standing at my bedroom door. "I am sorry to wake you like this. There has been another attack."

"What? Are they okay?" I ask.

"The victims are at the medical center," Army replies matter-of-factly.

I nod my head in reply, and to wake myself up. "Okay. I'll be ready in a few minutes."

"Sí. I will start the truck and meet you outside."

Searching for my clothes in the dark, I strike my shin on the bed. A muffled "Ouch" comes from my mouth.

Karen covers her head with a pillow. "Dan, I heard what Army said. Turn the light on and do what you need to. Hope everyone is fine."

"Thank you," I reply, flipping on the light switch. Locating my clothes, putting them on, and stepping out of the bedroom while turning off the light as I go, I meet Army in the Trailblazer in under five minutes.

"Good morning, Sunshine." Army's broad smile is evident, even in the dark.

Sarcastically, I reply, "Don't start. Yours is *not* the face I want to wake up to."

Army chuckles, puts the car in gear, and pulls out onto the dark, deserted street.

"I forgot to ask. You said victims, so more than one. How many are there, and do you know who they are?"

"Sí. You also know them."

I knit my brows together and search my memory of people I've met.

"Do not try so hard, amigo. It is Alejo and Victor."

"How bad are they hurt?"

"I am not sure. The nurse practitioner at the clinic called me."

The medical center is a one-story, cement-block building. A double glass front door stands behind a heavy wrought iron gate, which is locked. Army rings the bell. A petite, forty-some-year-old woman heads down the corridor and lets us in.

"¡Buenos días, Ms. Lopez! This is my partner and friend, Dan." I extend my hand to her, and she replies, "Buenos días. Come in. I locked the door because I am alone and in the back of the building."

We step into a small windowless waiting room. I smell antiseptics. Dilapidated plastic chairs are grouped randomly around the room. Despite the low-light room, I can still see the cracked vinyl flooring. Looking at Army, Ms. Lopez continues, "Comisario, I am sorry to wake you. The men . . . were attacked. *This* is no accidente. They were able to drive here and use the phone to call the after-hours number."

Army sighs. "How bad are they?"

Ms. Lopez talks over her shoulder as she leads us down the corridor. "Victor has a concussion. Someone hit him on the back of the head, *hard*. Alejo was attacked by something that left deep claw marks on his arm and his chest."

Army and I exchange glances. This feels too familiar.

"Are either of them awake?" I ask.

"Sí, Alejo is," she responds, opening the door to an exam room. She excuses herself to check on Victor.

The room has an exam table, two weather-worn chairs, and a tiny medicine chest. Bare-chested Alejo is sitting on the exam table and looks up when we walk in. There are bandages on his right bicep and another covering more than half his chest. Both have droplets of blood soaked through. His face is pale and drawn.

Army nods to him. "Can you tell me what happened?"

Alejo reaches for what's left of his shirt lying next to him.

Army stops him. "I am sorry, but I will need yours and Victor's clothes for evidence. I have some spare things in the truck for you to wear home."

Alejo nods, but puts little effort into it. He speaks in slow, breathy sentences with staggered pauses, "Victor and I drove out to the mill . . . I had walked away from the car when I heard Victor cry out. I turned to see what had happened. . . . Something attacked me. I think I put my arm up because suddenly I felt a terrible pain in it . . . The next thing I knew I was on the ground, and my chest felt like it was burning. I was screaming, kicking, and found a rock to hit it with. . . . It must have run off. I crawled to Victor, got him into the truck, and drove here. Is he all right?"

Army says, "Ms. Lopez is with him. What were you doing out there at this time of the night?"

Defiantly, Alejo raises his head. "Well, I learned that Eva and Karen were checking out the old mill for items for the hacienda. I wanted to see what was there. I am deeply invested in this project. I cannot have them putting in junk just because it is 'old.'"

I'm starting to feel my empathy wane a bit. He's a jerk.

"So, you were attempting to trespass on Emilio's property," Army replies. "You understand that is illegal."

"I did not do anything wrong. I never got onto his property. I am a victim! So, what are you going to do, Comisario?" he spits out angrily.

"You are right." Army sighs. "Can you describe who attacked you?"

"I am not sure it was a who. I heard animal noises, so I thought that maybe Emilio had dogs guarding the property. When I heard Victor yell, I turned, and there was something all black there. It clawed me. I did not see a face or anything. Just blackness."

Ms. Lopez knocks before stepping into the room. "Comisario, Victor is awake. Just be gentle when you question him. I am worried about the head injury."

"I'll have further questions for you at a later date." Army says to Alejo.

We head to the next exam room. Victor is sitting in a chair, head bandaged. "Hola, Comisario." Ms. Lopez and I stand near the door.

Army stoops down next to him. "Hola. Can you tell me what happened?"

Victor rubs his forehead. "I am not sure of it all. I remember driving Alejo to the old mill. We both got out of the car. He asked me to keep watch. Suddenly, someone hit me from the back. I do not remember anything after that until I woke up here."

"Victor, did you see anyone on the road? Other vehicles? Did you pass anyone?" I interject.

"I do not think so. It was late and very dark." Victor drops his head into his hands. Army pats him on the back. "Let's get you two home."

CHAPTER 14

I wake up as I feel Karen slide her arm across my chest. "Good morning," I whisper.

"Good morning. What happened?" she asks.

"Alejo and Victor were attacked last night. We got them and their truck home around five this morning. I'm hoping Army and I can look at the crime scene today."

"Well, sorry, but Army left the house about an hour ago. I heard the Trailblazer leave."

My head snaps around. "What? What time is it?"

"Nine thirty," Karen replies.

Sighing, I close my eyes and will myself to calm down. *Breathe in, breathe out. Army is my friend.* Repeat. "I'm gonna take a shower."

"Before you get up, I have to tell you about this dream I had," Karen starts. "I was at the hacienda, and I was calling for Eva when I noticed this young woman in the courtyard. I asked if I could help her. She said that her name was Ana María, and she was so happy to see how beautiful everything was. It looked as if the renovations were complete. I went to investigate the living room when Ana María started screaming of the danger there and ran across the street. I tried to follow her, but a motorcycle raced past and the driver pointed a finger at me. It frightened me, so I jumped back. Suddenly, there were so many race cars, motorcycles, and semis that sped by, I couldn't get across. That's when I woke up."

I pull Karen close. "I'm sorry you had such a bad dream. Whaddaya think it means?"

Shrugging her shoulders, Karen cuddles into me. "I don't know. Maybe working at the hacienda reminds me that Ana María will never see how beautiful it will be again, and that makes me sad."

"You sure you want to continue working there?"

"Yes, I am. Just knowing about her situation is sad, whether I work on the project or not. I'd like to see it through, if possible."

"Okay, then I'm good with it," I say, kissing her.

"Great." Karen nods. "I'll meet you in the kitchen."

Showered, dressed, and using positive self-talk about this situation, I head for the kitchen. The smell of freshly brewed coffee helps lift my spirits.

Eva and Karen are talking about a second trip to the old sugar mill to explore the remaining buildings. Placing her hand on my arm, Eva looks at me. "Army was afraid you would be upset that he left without you, but he wanted you to sleep in since this is your vacation."

I smile to reassure Eva, but I'm not happy about being left out of the investigation, *again*.

A few minutes later, Army arrives home. "I am sorry, my friend, I know you wanted to see the scene from last night, but I have taken enough of your vacation time."

I decide to let the situation rest for now. This is my friend. "Did you find anything at the scene?" I ask.

Whispering, he replies, "Not much. I took pictures and collected some evidence that I need to talk to you about later." In a louder voice, he says, "Today is about being a tourist and spending time with our beautiful, patient, and loving wives." He rubs his nose against Eva's.

"Gracias, mi amor. ¡Perfecto!" She giggles. "I was able to reach the caretaker at the restored hacienda, and he will let us in at one o'clock today. We should leave soon so we have enough time to get there."

The dry countryside rolls by. Dust devils fly up, and gravel dings the Trailblazer. I watch the landscape, architecture, and the colors all around. Karen reaches over and takes my hand. She is happy about being together, and so am I, except there is something about last night that isn't right. I can't figure it out. I replay what I remember repeatedly.

"We are here," Army announces, which serves to stop my ruminating over the details. Getting out of the truck, I hear Karen gasp. "This is amazing. It's better that I could have imagined."

The building is a deep coral color with bright-white painted wood trim around the entrance and weathered wood around the windows. I don't know if the colors are traditional, but it is strikingly beautiful.

I agree with her, it is stunning. Karen grabs the camera while Eva introduces us to a frail, elderly-looking man. Powder-white hair, watery grey eyes, thin-framed with a slight limp, wearing threadbare denim coveralls and a faded red plaid shirt.

"This is Roberto. He looks after this place." We all shake his hand, which is warm, but boney. His smile is welcoming.

Eva and Karen follow Roberto into the hacienda. Karen snaps pictures, and Eva asks questions in Spanish and takes notes on Roberto's answers. Army and I take notes of the craftsman details and use of the technical points, such as the pump for the courtyard fountain, and lighting switches and plumbing. Eva and Karen linger outside, discussing plant types, color, height, texture, and meaning associated with each one. Eva takes detailed notes while Karen photographs and videotapes both the courtyard and the perimeter of the building. Karen's eyes dance as she talks about the gardens and the plan for the hacienda they're working on. Eva begins a list of possible plants.

Army slaps me on the back. "Oh, mi amigo, I see a great deal of work ahead of us."

"Shhhhhhh, maybe they won't notice us and give the projects to someone else to do," I whisper.

Army chuckles under his breath. A couple of hours pass quickly, and we are ready to leave. We thank Roberto for his time and expertise.

Eva's phone rings, and she steps aside to answer. After a few minutes, she hangs up and says, "Karen, Marco called, and he would like to visit the hacienda tomorrow." Eva contacts Brad and arranges for him to also be there.

Once in the truck, Eva says, "They can both meet at 9:30 tomorrow morning." She touches Army's shoulder. "Could you please drop Karen and me off at the garden center? We would like to see what they have in stock and what needs to be ordered."

"Sí. Dan and I will stop at the station while you do that. Call when you are ready to go home. But first, something to eat, please."

We stop at a small family-run restaurant. The inside is dark, quiet, and cool, the perfect escape from the afternoon heat. Army exchanges a few words with the man that greets us at the door. "The man and his wife own this place, and his wife is also the cook. There is not a printed menu. He will tell us what is being served today, and then we can decide what we each want."

After several exchanges of rapid Spanish, Army turns to us. "There are deep-fried shredded chicken tacos or red chilies and pork stew. All come with rice and beans."

Karen and Eva opt for the fried tacos. Army and I order the pork stew. Although it is in Spanish, I figure out that Army is also ordering guacamole, salsa, chips, and a pitcher of margaritas. Once lunch is ordered, Eva brings out her notepad. "That hacienda was amazing. I'm excited to take some of the ideas back and see if they work at our site."

Karen snorts a laugh. "I am too, except I think we just came up with a bunch more projects for Brad to do."

Eva glances sideways at Army and me. "Or husbands."

Giggling, Karen replies, "Good idea. They work inexpensively."

"Whose idea was it to come here?" I say, looking at Army. He smiles and shrugs his shoulders.

The guacamole, salsa, and chips arrive, but I'm most excited about the pitcher of lime margaritas. They're sweet, cold, and wet with a tang at the back of my throat. They slide down with ease. Talking, laughing, and reminiscing with Karen and these two good friends makes me appreciate this time in my life. I remind myself that these are my friends, I'm here on vacation, and memories like today last longer than any investigation. We tuck into our lunches and another pitcher. I could stay here for hours, but soon we are back on the road. I'm content with how today went and for these people.

The garden center is at the edge of town. Karen and Eva leave with the camera and notepad, then Army and I head to the station.

Removing the bags from the evidence lockup, Army lays Alejo's and Victor's clothing out on the desk. "Victor's shirt and pants have dirt on the front of them, so he must have fallen forward when he was hit," he states.

"And Alejo's have some serious rips on both the chest and the arm. It looks like blood. We should test it to make sure it's only Alejo's. If we're lucky, the attacker was injured and their blood is on there too."

"I plan to have it all tested at the lab in Guadalajara. I found some blood drops at the scene, so I will send those too." Army shoots me a sideways glance. "I am worried about who is doing this and why."

"Hopefully when we find out the who, then we find out the why," I reply. "Let's see what this evidence tells us. Then it'll be good old-fashioned police work mixed with a bit of luck." Looking between the photos of the scene, the victims' injuries, and the clothing, there's something not right, but what?

"Army, do you notice anything wrong, or missing, or out of place here?"

"No. Everything looks just as Alejo described. The claw marks in the shirt line up with his injuries. I double-checked. I even checked to make sure Victor had a bump on his head. He does, and it's big, along with a cut. Someone hit him really hard. They were making sure he was knocked out. Why? What's bothering you?"

"I'm not sure. This is bad, like the Juan Mercado scene. I know there should be something more, but I can't think of what it is."

Army's phone rings. "Sí. Bueno." He hangs up. "The wives are ready to be picked up." He locks up the evidence again and secures the office.

Karen and Eva are waiting outside of the garden center. They climb in and are happily chatting about possible purchases of plants and yard accessories to fit their designs.

Entering the kitchen at home, Eva asks, "Is anyone hungry?"

In slow-motion unison, Karen, Army, and I shake our heads. Eva laughs out loud. "Okay, maybe later we can snack on leftovers."

"Dan, I'm going to change clothes and freshen up," Karen says. "I need to ask your opinion on something."

I follow her into the bedroom. "What's up?" I ask.

"When Eva and I were at the garden center, Eva was talking to the supervisor about ordering some plants. I started wandering around and stopped to look at some trees. That's when I heard someone crying, so I peeked around the trees. Valeria was crying, and José Luis was comforting her. The way they were touching was not in an 'I'm a friend' way. It was much more intimate."

"Who's Valeria again?"

"The young pregnant girl at Ana María's funeral who Emilio was yelling at."

"Could you hear what they were saying?"

She shakes her head. "Not all of it, and my Spanish is not as good as yours. From the way she was pulling on his arm, I got the feeling she was pleading with him for something."

"So, what did he do?"

"He pulled her hands off his arm and shoved her away. I heard him say, 'Ahora, no,' or 'Not now,' and something like 'This is not a good time.' He walked away and left her standing there, crying. She went into one of the greenhouses. I found out from Eva that Valeria works there."

"Curioser and curioser. I'll talk to Army about what you saw. My concern is that José Luis had something to do with his wife's death, but why? An affair? Unwanted pregnancy? Or her money with a new young wife, Valeria, and baby?" I need to figure this out.

CHAPTER 15

Army leans into Eva and kisses her, then lets her know about our day. We are taking evidence to the crime lab and stopping at a couple of the processing plants just to be sure there is no new activity.

He grabs his keys and places his hand on the doorknob. "I want to make sure we have everything in the truck we might need today."

We step out onto the driveway, then freeze. Ernesto is on the sidewalk staring at us. He makes eye contact with me, then moves toward us, bleats, turns, takes two steps, and bleats again.

I look at Army, who appears as puzzled as I do. I question, "Don't tell me he wants us to follow him."

Army shrugs. "Sadly, it will not be the strangest thing I have done in my career. ¡Àndale!" He waves us forward.

We fall in line behind Ernesto, who trots several feet in front of us until we reach the hacienda. Ernesto releases a loud bleat, then turns and saunters away down the street.

The door is slightly ajar. I know that Eva would've locked up before leaving. A sense of foreboding descends over me. Anxiously, I whisper to Army, "Did you bring a gun?"

"I was following a goat. I didn't think I would need one," he responds quietly, easing the door open further and stepping in.

I slide next to him, and we check both sides of the courtyard. He raises his fist in the police signal of 'hold,' then indicates the next step. Pointing to the left for me, and himself the right. Just like old times.

A door slams on the other side of the house. Army runs in that direction, and I'm about to follow him when I notice a crumpled form near the fountain in the center of the courtyard. A few steps closer, I find Brad Carpenter, dead. He's lying on his left side, eyes open, right hand clenched shut and his throat slashed. I check for a pulse. Nothing. I start an initial survey of the area for possible evidence.

Army hurries back in. "Is he dead?" I nod affirmatively. He sighs. "Come help me. Marco is outside and unconscious."

Marco, the art dealer, is lying on his back on the ground, blood oozing from the side of his face. Army calls for help as I lean down to examine him. He groans and reaches his hand to his forehead.

"Lie still," I instruct. "Help is on the way. I'm going to look for some kind of towel."

Marco waves me off. "No, I'm fine."

"Okay, then what happened?"

Sighing, Marco looks at me and appears to be trying to focus. "I'm not sure. Where am I?"

"Outside the hacienda. It appears you were attacked. What do you remember seeing?" I question.

"That's right, I have an appointment to meet Eva and Karen

here today." He touches his head. "I came early to look at the place when suddenly someone came running out and knocked me down. I don't remember what happened then."

I push for more. "Did you see who it was?"

"I don't know anyone else in town. I remember something black, but not a face." I survey the alley, looking for anything that may have been dropped in the altercation. Only Marco's briefcase lays next to him.

An ambulance arrives, and Army brings them to Marco. I head back inside to survey the scene.

Army returns a short time later. "Whoever was here got away." He looks down at the body. "I will go home and bring the truck back. We need to process the scene. And I'll let Karen and Eva know they cannot work here today. Please stay with the body."

I nod in acknowledgement. After Army leaves, I search the interior of the hacienda for anything out of place or missing. Nothing I can see.

Minutes later, he's back with the evidence kit, camera, and other crime scene equipment. Pictures are taken of the area. The coroner's van arrives, and the attendants speak to Army and turn the body over. Deep slash marks across his throat have severed his carotid artery. With gloves on, I bag Brad's hands to preserve any evidence. Army swabs the wounds for particulates and individually bags and tags them. "Did you get a photograph of this partial shoe print?"

"Yeah. Right heel, right corner missing," I say.

He nods. "The amount of blood here indicates that this is where he was killed."

"We must have just missed it by minutes. None of the blood has dried, even with it being very warm in here. I took samples of the pooled blood."

The coroner's assistants remove the body. We photograph and fingerprint surfaces around the hacienda, including the back door our mystery person exited from.

"Nothing," Army says. "No prints. Either the killer was wearing gloves or had time to wipe down the surfaces before we showed up."

"There should be prints of Eva, Karen, you, and myself on several of the door handles. So my guess is they were wiped," I reply.

"Let's get the evidence back to the office and catalog it." We pack everything into the truck and ride in silence to the station. Once there, the evidence unloaded and recorded, I ask, "What was Brad doing there so early? It wasn't even 9:00 a.m."

"I noticed his motorcycle parked on the side of the house. My first thought was that he was still working on something, or he may have even been meeting someone other than Eva and Karen. But how did he get in? I know Eva did not give him a key."

"If he arrived and someone was already inside, then he would have just walked in. Either way, he must not have been concerned since his killer got very close."

"Or he was caught by surprise," Army adds. "This is getting dangerous. What is this killer after?"

"Can you think of anything the two victims have in common?" I look to Army, who shakes his head.

He picks up his keys to the truck. "Come, amigo. Let us get home to our wives. We can have a late supper and look at the evidence tomorrow."

"What? We're in the middle of *another* murder investigation. I think we should stay and go over the evidence."

"And *I* think that the evidence can wait for a day," Army replies.

What is going on? Repeat to self, "This is not my investigation, this is my friend."

I bow my head in acquiescence, though the ride home is quiet.

Opening the door to the kitchen, I am suddenly hungry. Army and I haven't eaten all day. The smell of spices and cooked meat fills the air. "What are we having?" I ask.

Pulling the lid off a slow cooker, Eva smiles. "Pork carnitas."

"I have no clue what that is." I look from Eva to Karen and back.

Karen giggles. "Pulled pork, Mexican-style. Sara made an entire pot full. She also dropped off tortillas, which we've been warming in the oven."

"Karen, we need to do something special for Sara," I say. "Her kindness is greatly appreciated."

Karen nods.

"No, you don't," Eva replies. "She is having fun using the olive oils and balsamic vinegars that came in the gift basket you brought here."

Karen looks at the clock. "You guys are pretty late. It's dark outside. I feel so bad, Brad killed and Marco hurt. Any idea who did this?"

Army sighs. "No, I do not have any suspects. I am so sorry. This is not a vacation for either of you. I wanted it to be more fun. Mis disculpas."

Karen is the first to respond. "Don't feel bad. I know this is not the vacation you planned for us, but seeing both of you has been fun."

"Thank you," Army says, bowing his head. "You are too kind. I promise that we will do some vacation things before you leave."

We take places at the table. Eva fills plates with helpings of meat and passes side dishes of tortillas, rice, beans, and guacamole.

"Any idea when we'll be able to get into the hacienda?" Karen asks.

"I'm sorry, but I cannot let that happen for a few days. It's a crime scene," Army states without looking up from his plate.

Karen nods understanding. "I get it. Eva and I plan to go back to the mill tomorrow since we didn't get through all the buildings. Emilio will have someone meet us there. It'll give us something to work on. It does break my heart that Brad was killed. He was a gifted artist."

A solemn mood descends as we eat. Thoughts run through my mind about the thread that ties these murders together . . . something seen or known? Who would have had contact with both? Did the victims know the danger they were in? A list forms in my head, then I realize that it could be any number of people in town. Worse is that many are Army's family. My eyes travel to Army, who is happily finishing eating. I hope my friend will not have to make a difficult choice, or hasn't already.

Donna Rewolinski

I help put away leftovers. Once the kitchen is cleaned, Karen and Eva sit at the table looking through photos of the hacienda, trying to make notes on possible projects. I can hear their sadness at not having Brad to help make them happen.

"I know we are all saddened by Brad's death, but we need to do something this evening," Army says. "There is a band playing at the Hotel del Sol. Come, let us go."

We step out of the house and into a wonderful night. The air is warm with a slight breeze, but not cold. Approaching the hotel, upbeat music, laughter, and talking radiates into the street. The hotel is a two-story adobe building painted a soft tangerine color, and a bronzed Aztec sun sits above the exterior arch. Stepping under the arch, we enter a Spanish garden with a white, ornate, four-tiered fountain shaped like a budding flower in the center. Walkways lead past trimmed, green hedges and spectacular flower beds to the entrance of the hotel and banquet hall. The hall is painted a paler version of the exterior color. It has polished, black, marble floors, and a dark wooden bar occupies the back wall. A small dance floor sits in front of the bandstand. Tables and chairs are crammed inside and about sixty-percent filled. A five-piece band fills the room with music.

Army secures an open table. The music is infectious, and I find myself dancing up to the bar for the first round. After giving my order to the bartender, I make eye contact with Pedro, who's lounging at the end of the counter. The noise level in the room decreases as the band takes a break. I approach Pedro, and we shake hands. "What can I get you to drink, Mr. Mayor?"

144

He laughs. "Cerveza, gracias. How is your investigation going?"

"Not mine. Army's. I'm just helping where I can."

"I am glad he has someone helping him." Pedro's eyes don't hold the warmth that sentiment would typically imply. *What's that about? Does he has a motive in all of this?*

"It must be a tough job being the mayor," I say. Pedro shrugs, so I continue, "I'm sorry, but I couldn't help overhearing Emilio Mendoza yelling at you earlier this week."

Pedro suddenly stands straight up. "What did you hear?"

I play coy. "It wasn't so much the words, but the tone. Why was he so angry?"

His shoulders relax as a smirk crosses his lips. "When I ran for mayor, I promised there would be an increase in the amount of money coming into the town. Emilio was pointing that out to me."

"I thought I heard him say Juan Mercado's name, but I could be wrong."

"No, you are not wrong. Emilio feels that with Juan's death happening on the land for the new water park, other sites should now be considered and the one best for the town be picked. I disagree, so he is very angry."

"The best site for the town or for Emilio?"

Pedro shrugs and takes a sip. "Thank you for the cerveza. Excuse me, I see someone I must speak with."

I nod understanding and take the rest of the drinks back to the table. Army asks, "What were you talking to Pedro about?"

"Just asking if Emilio revealed anything new when he was in the office the other day."

"And?"

"Nothing, or at least nothing he can talk about."

Karen breaks in, "Dan, come dance with me, please."

Karen and I venture onto the dance floor, and Army and Eva join us. I'm not sure if what I'm doing passes as dancing, but twenty minutes of twirling, twisting, and hopping from foot to foot has my heart rate and spirits up. Sitting back at the table, we're laughing and having a second round. The band takes another break, but in the lull, angry voices can be heard nearby. Everyone's head is on a swivel trying to determine where the ruckus is coming from. Army gets on his feet and moves toward the courtyard. I follow him. Exiting the door, I don't see anyone. Shoulder to shoulder, we head toward the voices that appear to be coming from the other side of the courtyard wall. Around the corner, Army runs into Victor.

Victor takes a step back and looks around, confused. "Todo bien?"

Sighing, Army replies, "I heard people arguing. Were you talking to someone, or did you see anyone else?"

"I just arrived. There were two men who got into a truck and left as I was coming up the walk."

"Who were they?" I question.

"I did not see. It was dark," he replies.

Victor walks toward the hall. Army looks up and down the parking lot and rubs his chin. I ask, "Did you hear any of what was said?"

"Only pieces of it, like 'The job is done,' 'I want money.' I did not recognize the voices."

What job? An employer who's slow to pay, or something more sinister?

"Is everything okay?" Karen's voice interrupts my thoughts. She's standing behind us.

"Yes," Army and I reply in unison. Army motions to the door. "Let us go back inside," he states, then walks toward the hotel.

Eva and Victor have added two more chairs next to ours. "Sara will be coming soon. She is closing the store," Victor tells us.

I grab Army's arm and look around. "What do you think it means? 'The job is done' could mean that with Juan Mercado's death, the site of the water park is in question. That benefits Emilio. Brad's death hinders the completion of the hacienda, and not everyone wanted it finished."

"Of course, the cattle rustling is still happening. That could be the job. Patience, mi amigo. This is not the time or place. Let us enjoy this evening," Army slaps me on the back.

I'm uneasy, and my coppy senses tingle that this was significant. Several minutes later, Sara arrives. Rounds of drinks, laughter, and conversation fill the rest of the evening. I do my best to let it go, but something nags at the back of my brain.

CHAPTER 16

The sun is barely up, but I'm awake. Dressed, I head for the kitchen to start the morning coffee. Openings in the curtains allow slits of sunshine to create bars of light on the floor and add a soft glow to the room. As my eyes trace the light across the floor and reach the back door, I notice an envelope partially under it. Picking it up, I notice that it's addressed to Army and, more importantly, not sealed. I mentally wrestle with respecting Army's privacy versus satisfying my curiosity and seeing what's inside. I swivel my head from side to side and over both shoulders, then slide the contents out onto the kitchen table. I catch my breath, frozen where I stand. Pictures of Karen, Eva, and myself at the Hotel del Sol with red bullseyes drawn over each of us. A note flutters out, saying, 'No escuchaste nuestras advertencias.' I use my phone to translate. It says, 'You didn't listen to our warnings.' I finally exhale, and my brain starts to whir. If this has happened before, it would explain why Army has been reluctant to involve me in the investigations. I drop my arms. The tension and animosity I felt towards him dissipate as I stare at the photos.

"What are you doing?" from across the room brings me

back. I look up to see Army standing about five feet in front of me, arms across his chest, eyes glaring. Obviously aware that I've opened the envelope.

"I'm sorry, my friend. I needed to know what was going on," I stammer.

"No! You did not," Army snaps. "You need to trust me as your former partner, but more importantly as your friend." He glares, legs shoulder-width apart, and refuses to break eye contact. A very defensive stance.

Holding up my hands and dropping my shoulders, I say, "You're absolutely right. But we've been through a lot as partners *and* friends. I don't think anyone else in town has your back. I do."

"No! You are a guest in my house, as is Karen. You are not a cop down here. I cannot risk anyone else being hurt. This is my job."

Army and I both jump as Karen enters the kitchen, saying, "No, Army. You and Dan need to solve this. I don't like bullies, and I won't stand by and let them win."

Eva quietly comes and stands by Army. I show her and Karen the photos.

Eva lays her hand on Army's arm. "You give Karen and me very little credit. We are cops' wives and have been for a long time. We have always known the danger when you leave the house. I agree with Karen. Do not let the criminals force you to look the other way. If you do, then it is time to stop being Comisario General. You work for the victims."

Army drops his head, releases a long, deep sigh, then laughs. "I am outnumbered."

Eva kisses Army's cheek. "Mi amor, you have it wrong. We four are a team!"

Army searches each of our faces. We nod in agreement. "Okay, then you are all part of the investigations. I want each of you to be very careful and safe. Never be alone, please. The idea of you all being involved does not make me happy."

I slap Army on the back. "Where do we begin?"

"We need to review the evidence collected so far. I have it all locked up at the station. After breakfast, we can go there."

Karen turns toward me. "Dan, we could do what we did in Ireland."

I roll my eyes up and back, trying to understand what she means. "Solve the murder?"

"Well, there was that, but I was thinking of the murder board Quinn, the Irish officer we worked with, had at home. The four of us can look at the evidence and give out ideas."

Army shakes his head. "I am not comfortable with the evidence being here after the attempted break-in."

"Quinn didn't have the original evidence. Just copies," Karen retorts.

Army swivels his head between me and Karen. "He let you see everything?"

"Karen referred to it as 'Clue.' Once an investigator, always an investigator. That goes for the one I live with." All eyes turn to Karen, who grins back.

"Okay, I will bring copies home, then we can all work together." Army's voice has a touch of defeat in it.

Karen brightens up. "Last time, we used a blank wall. Is

there one in the spare room? Even if people visit, they won't see it if we keep the door closed."

Army rubs his head as Eva says, "Mi amor, it will work out." She gently kisses his forehead. "Who is ready for breakfast?"

Feeling the release of the negative thoughts regarding my friend lifts my spirit and improves my appetite. I dig into breakfast. Conversation is filled with energy and laughter.

When we're finished, Army and I head to the station to copy the evidence. I have brought two empty backpacks. Once there, Army pulls out boxes and boxes. "Currently, we are dealing with several crimes: two murders, Ana María's death, the attacks on Victor, Alejo, and Marco, as well as the cattle rustling."

"Don't forget the attack on you, too," I add.

Army waves a hand dismissively. "I think that when one of the other crimes is solved, the evidence will lead to the attack on me. I am not worried about that. Others hurt or dead concern me."

"Let's copy one at a time. I'll put the copies in the backpacks I brought, in case someone is watching."

"Good idea. I do not want to tempt anyone with the thought that the evidence is at my home."

Copying takes longer than expected, and my legs and feet are starting to hurt from standing at the copy machine. My shoulders ache from the redundant motion of putting items on and taking them off the copier, but finally, it's done. Army and I step out of the office, each with a bag that gets loaded into the Trailblazer, and we head home.

After lunch, the four of us are organizing the evidence copies in a spare bedroom at Army's house. I'm not sure who is more excited about the investigation, Karen or Eva. Precision and efficiency dominate the arranging of the evidence.

Karen steps back to survey the work so far. "Right now, we have Ana María's death and the two murders up on the board, and we still have several bags to do. We're gonna need more than one wall. Also, big sheets of paper to write on and a lot of markers. I get the feeling that many of these crimes are interrelated."

"I think you are right, amiga," Eva says, crossing her arms across her chest. "I am sure many of these acts involve the same people, but who and how many?" She removes a painting of a cowboy on a horse and places it behind the dresser. "We can use this wall, too."

"Army, we need to get the clothing, photos, lab reports, and other evidence from the attacks and Brad's murder to the crime lab," I say, looking at Army. He nods, but appears mesmerized by what is on the wall before him.

"Army, do you see something?" Karen inquires.

"No . . . I'm just getting a feeling that this is all intertwined, which is a scary thought. Who is so evil to have done these things?"

Eva kisses Army's cheek. "I do not know, but I think, no, I believe that together we can stop them."

"I think we should put the investigation aside for now. Eva, you said that Sara owns a grocery store. Would she have markers?" Karen asks.

"I don't know, but we could walk over," Eva replies. "Let's go and decide what we want for dinner."

Skepticism creeps into my voice. "In the middle of several major investigations, we're gonna stop and take a walk?"

With an incredulous look, Karen says, "Yes, Dan. We're stepping away from the evidence for now. We'll return to it with fresh eyes when we get back."

"O-okay," I say, looking at Army, who's trying his best not to laugh. "Are you laughing?"

"No, my friend, I would never laugh at you," he replies with a broad grin.

"Yeah, and I don't believe you," I reply sarcastically.

Army bursts out laughing. "Come, let us walk. We are with good friends and beautiful women."

Conversation switches to topics of what to have for dinner and snacks this evening. Karen grabs my hand as we go, and Eva and Army do the same with each other. I relax and breathe deeply. Dust flies up, and withered weeds fill the cracks in the sidewalks. As we pass doorways, the dry air carries mouthwatering scents of dinners being prepared. My stomach tells my investigator brain to think about food, not crime.

A small bell over the door chimes as we step in. Sara's store is one large room with shelves around the perimeter and another set of shelves in the center. She stands behind a small counter, which holds an antiquated cash register, near the entrance and greets us. "¡Hola, amigos! Welcome. How can I help you?"

Army stops and talks with her while Eva and Karen discuss meal ideas. I take the opportunity to explore her inventory. Bottles of juice, soda, canned beans, vegetables, soups, loaves of bread, boxed crackers, cookies, and cold cereals dominate, but there's only instant coffee. Where are Eva and

Army getting their fresh ground coffee? Maybe they have it delivered. Intrigued by the unfamiliar names and packaging, I take items off the shelves and examine them when two middle-aged women enter the store. Sara acknowledges them as they turn down one of the aisles. They each pick up a can of vegetables and appear to be reading the label, then giggle and nudge each other while stealing glances at Sara. My curiosity piqued, I step closer and catch some of the whispered words. "Esposo . . . tiene un amante . . . Carlota." More giggling.

Are my suspicions correct that Victor and Carlota are having an affair? The two women put the cans back on the shelf and wave goodbye to Sara, but the giggling continues until they leave. Sara either doesn't notice or has an amazing poker face. Eva and Karen bring their items to the counter, Sara rings them up, and Eva pays while Sara bags the groceries. Army hugs her. "¡Adiós, hermana!"

"I am sorry I did not have the markers you wanted. Gracias. ¡Buenas tardes!" she responds. Army and I each grab a grocery-filled plastic bag and we all head back.

Once home, the items are laid out. Army and I have volunteered to cook tonight. I butter a loaf of crusty bread and place it in the oven, and Army heads out to heat up the grill.

I stand at the counter chopping vegetables for a salad. *This town has several subtexts. I wish I knew which are important and which are rumor and innuendo. How do I find out without insulting my friend?*

"Dan." Karen's voice gets my attention.

"What?"

"If you rip that lettuce any smaller, it'll be shredded."

"Sorry, my mind wandered. I have a few more things to chop up and get into the bowl, then I'll see if Army needs help on the grill."

Karen leans into me and kisses my cheek.

Salad complete and bread warming, I head outside to check on how the meat is doing. "Looks good," I say. "Hey, who were the two women that came into Sara's store?"

"Pffft" escapes Army's mouth as he rolls his eyes. "Those are the Garcia sisters. They never married, and their main job has always been to spread rumors, true or not."

"They seemed to giggle about something the entire time."

"Take little stock in anything you hear from them," Army says. "I think these are done." He places the meat on a platter and heads for the house with me right behind.

Eva places the salad bowl on the table. "I spoke to Emilio, and he understands that with Brad's death, Karen and I must rethink the projects. We want to go to the old mill before it gets too dark."

Army turns toward her. "Dan and I can go, too."

"I don't think there is a reason you have to. Karen and I need to look at things, and it may take some time. We will be careful. You and Dan stay here and relax."

"I think it is best if I go with," Army insists.

Eva turns toward him, lowering her voice. "I will not live in fear. We will be *fine*."

Army's voice is low and deliberate. "You and Karen being alone at the old place does *not* make me happy."

"I understand that, but we are still going," Eva states, looking directly and firmly at Army.

Army responds with a sigh and throws his hands up. We finish eating, then he and I clean up, put the food away, and move to the 'Evidence Room.'

Blank paper under each crime begs for theories, suspects, and a resolution.

"Okay, so let's start with ideas of who would benefit from each crime," I throw out. "Ana María's death would be her husband and maybe her brother-in-law, Emilio."

Army writes down both names. "Juan Mercado's death could be Emilio if the location of the water park moves to his piece of land." He puts Emilio's name there too.

"Everything else, I'm lost for suspects. What about you?" I ask.

"There are always theories of profit or to eliminate witnesses or people in the way, but I have no suspects." Army is rubbing his hand over his chin when his phone rings. "¿Qué? Sí. ¡Quédate donde estás, no te muevas y no toques nada!"

Anxiety shoots through my body. "What's up? Who was that?"

Army speaks through a clenched jaw. "That was Eva. She and Karen went to the mill and were walking through one of the buildings. She says there is a pool of something dark and flies buzzing around. She's not sure what it is, so she called me."

"Are they all right?"

"Sí. ¡Vámonos!"

Several minutes later, the Trailblazer pulls up next to the mill. Karen and Eva are standing outside one of the outbuildings with a man I haven't met.

"This is Carlos. He works for Emilio. It's in there." Karen points toward the door.

Army and I step inside a small wooden plank building. The pool covers an area roughly four feet long by three feet wide. One whiff of the stale iron smell tells me it's blood, but from what?

"Amigo, we need to process this scene. This is blood, and nothing survives that has lost this much. I do not see remains of an animal, if that was what was truly killed here."

Tension rises up my neck. "The claw marks on the floor and walls are deep. Something was very angry. We'll have to send samples to the crime lab and let them determine if it is human or animal."

We ask Karen, Eva, and Carlos to wait near the truck, then grab the crime scene equipment from it. Back inside, I swab the floor and walls and bag the evidence. Army takes photographs. There are quite a bit of discarded garbage items, such as cups, paper, chewing gum, plastic soda bottles, and cigarette butts. All are retrieved, bagged, and tagged. Slowly, we make our way around the room. Materials are secured in the truck to be cataloged.

I give the room one last sweep and examine the claw marks more closely. "Hey, Army. These marks look familiar to me. Could they be the same on our victim Juan Mercado? What if this is where he was killed? Could look bad for Emilio."

"Dan, now you are the one jumping to conclusions. If Mr. Mercado was killed here, that doesn't mean Emilio was involved."

We are making a last sweep of the scene when Emilio

shows up in a BMW sedan and parks next to the truck. He jumps out of the driver's side as it jerks to a stop, then heads for Army, his face so red he could pop a blood vessel at any moment. "What are you doing? I did not give permission for the policia to search on *my* land." His employee must have called him about the situation. Carlos has disappeared since we arrived. Why?

A smirk slides across Army's face, then disappears. "We are investigating a possible crime scene."

"Crime scene? What crime?" Emilio throws up his hands. "You policia are always looking for something where there is nothing."

"There appears to be a suspicious blood pool on the floor of one of *your* buildings."

Emilio stomps to the building and throws open the door. "This spot near the door? I am sure it is nothing. An animal killed another animal, or maybe gave birth here. Estúpido. There is not a crime here. Get off my land." He slams the door shut.

"You do not wish to know the truth?" Army asks quietly.

"I know the truth. You can leave." Emilio stands with his feet planted and his arms across his chest.

Army bows his head. "As you wish. Everyone, let's go."

Karen, Eva, and I climb into the Trailblazer with Army, and we head home.

"You're still going to send the samples into the crime lab, right?" I ask.

A grin creases Army's face. "Of course."

"One of the reasons I like you." We all laugh.

CHAPTER 17

Last night, Army and I secured the additional evidence at the station, copied what we could, and came home to add it to the walls. This morning as I pass the doorway of the 'murder room,' I stop in my tracks as I hear Karen and Eva discussing theories of how to commit murder and cover up the crime with enough confidence to make me uneasy. Sticking my head into the room, I say, "Planning the demise of Army or myself?"

"Both" comes the unified response, followed by giggling.

"You two make me nervous," I reply.

Karen shrugs. "Dan, you and Army married smart women with strong opinions, but you're loved. We'd never hurt you."

"Good to know. Any ideas on who did what when?" I ask.

Eva shakes her head. "No, but I am sure that just one piece of information or evidence will be the thread that connects things together. I wish we knew if it is one person or more who did these terrible things."

"Yeah, that would be nice to know. I'll make coffee," I say, then wander into the kitchen. Army joins me at the table. "Today, we will take the evidence to the crime lab. I received a text that the results of the trace evidence from the scene of Juan Mercado's death are in."

"Let's hope there's something there that gives us a lead."

Karen and Eva sit at the table with us. Karen picks up her cup of coffee. "Army, would Eva and I be able to get into the hacienda today?"

"Yes, I will release the scene this morning. I think Dan and I have processed it for all the evidence we are going to find."

"Brad's death was terrible," Eva states, looking between me and Army. "It is getting scary with everything. These murders, cattle rustling, and you being attacked, Army."

"You are right. I'm getting calls from people in town demanding answers. I have none," Army replies.

"Brad's nephew, Lad, called a few minutes ago. He said this town is the place his uncle was happiest. He will let us know when he has finished the funeral arrangements." Eva chokes up.

Army hugs Eva, and Karen and I nod. We have no words.

Sighing, Army replies, "I am doing my best job to solve all of this."

Eva closes her eyes and puts her head back. "I will be happy when the restoration is done. I feel that there has been a black cloud hanging over it from the beginning."

"The saddest part is that Brad touched so many places," Karen says. "It's going to be hard to put all his pieces in place without him.

"I will try to help, but solving these crimes comes first. I know that Victor has done some carpentry work in the past. I can ask him too," Army says.

"Don't leave me out. I can help," I chime in.

Eva smiles at us. Karen states, "I know that it takes you away from the investigations, but hopefully we'll only need you for a few hours."

"First, Dan and I are taking the evidence to Guadalajara. While we are gone, please make a list of projects to be done. If you can prioritize them, we can devise a plan when we get home, okay?"

Eva gives Army a kiss on the cheek. "Gracias, mi amor."

Breakfast finished, we head to the hacienda. I remove the police tape, and Karen and Eva start their walk-through. Army and I then head to the station, pick up the evidence, and drive to the crime lab.

Once there, Luis greets us. "¡Hola, amigos! ¿Cómo están?"

"¡Muy bien!" I reply.

"Good, good. I have the results of the tox screen. No drugs or any kind of alcohol in Mr. Mercado's system. He had the remains of a meal in his stomach. Beef, rice, and beans. He was killed within an hour or so afterwards. Nothing under his fingernails. He had a fresh manicure."

"There is no evidence at all?" Army remarks.

Luis grins. "My friend, I would not call you here for nothing. Particulates were found in the claw marks. Minute fibers from a sugar cane plant embedded in one of the wounds and on his clothes."

"If we found similar sugar cane fibers, does your lab have the capability to match them?" I ask. If we can, this might be the break we need.

"If they are from the same plant, yes. Plants have a DNA unique to each, same as people," Luis replies.

Army's eyes light up. "I think we should work on a warrant for Emilio's outbuilding." He extends his hand to Luis. "Thank you, my friend. Unfortunately, we have brought you and your staff more work. Have you begun the autopsy on Brad Carpenter?"

"Not yet. It has been busier than normal, but I have it scheduled for tomorrow. I will call you when I am done."

We drive in relative silence. I imagine Army is crafting the wording needed to obtain a search warrant for Emilio's building. Will the plant DNA lead us to Emilio as the murderer, and if it doesn't, where do we start looking for another suspect? I'm not sure I can even identify sugar cane. Also, I'm interested if the lab finds any prints from the garbage we collected, but can we tie it to the murders?

We arrive at the hacienda, and Karen and Eva walk us through the project.

"I think the biggest help would be to finish the kitchen. Brad built all the cabinets, so they just need to be delivered and installed," Eva states. "I felt bad calling Brad's nephew at this time, but he seemed anxious to get rid of the cabinets. He said he'd have them here tomorrow. Can you do it then?"

Army and I look at each other. Not what we had planned, but we agree to help.

Eva's eyes dance with joy. "Gracias."

"Once the kitchen is complete, the only big thing left is the exterior color and plants," Karen adds. "We'll need all the help we can get with that. I think Eva and I can handle most of the staging inside."

"That reminds me that I need to speak with Juan to order the paint," Eva says.

"Sounds like a plan. We can do that," I say and elbow Army to agree with me. He rolls his eyes.

"We should go home and have lunch. Are leftovers okay?" Eva asks.

"Leftovers sound great," I reply. "I'm starved."

Karen mutters under her breath, "That's a shock."

"Yeah, yeah." I laugh.

Sitting around the table, eating, laughing, and a couple of margaritas later, I'm feeling relaxed and glad to be here.

"Karen and I need to get back to the hacienda and do some touch-up painting before Marco brings in the furniture and accessories he found," Eva says.

"You need us to help?" I ask.

"If you could come, Dan, the fountain isn't working correctly," Karen replies.

"Yeah, I can look at it." I glance over at Army. "You gonna be okay on your own?"

"Sí, amigo. I have paperwork to finish, including payroll. I will drop you all off and then be at the station if you need me," he replies.

We head out. At the hacienda, I stop in the courtyard while Karen and Eva head inside. Once the door is opened, Eva stops so suddenly that Karen bumps into her.

"Alejo, what are you doing?" she says.

He jumps in place, nearly dropping the picture he's hanging. "This photograph is on loan from my father-in-law's collection of his father's victorious bullfights. It deserves proper presentation," he responds, returning to position it on the wall.

Eva places her hands on her hips. "No. This is to be a period-correct restoration. They did not have giant photographs. Get the metal eye hooks out. We just had the plaster walls repaired."

Alejo spins around. "You fail to appreciate the sizable contributions I have made to see the success of this project."

"How did you get in?" Eva asks.

"I will take my complaints to the rest of the committee. I also withdraw any future monetary support. Let us see how you do then. I will not be around to help with any of the labor as well."

"Labor? What labor have you helped with? Nothing! You have not done one bit of physical work here!" Eva yells as he turns toward the wall, then mutters in Spanish. I don't think the comments were complimentary.

Alejo grabs the photo and storms out, but trips on the wire hanging from the back of the picture. He falls against the doorframe before regaining his balance, then slams the door behind him. I look between Eva and Karen. Karen is snickering.

"Are you laughing at him?" I ask.

"Yes. I know that's mean, but he didn't get the dramatic exit he was hoping for. It couldn't have happened to a nicer guy," she replies sarcastically.

Eva has her hand over her mouth as her body shakes with repressed laughter until she can't contain it any longer and bursts. Karen joins in. Both double over. I snicker along with them.

Eva sighs and dabs her eyes for tears. "I needed that. This job has been very stressful."

"Come on, Eva. We can finish this without him," Karen says. "I'm curious how he got in. He gave me his keys a while back."

"Knowing that jerk, he gave you a copy of the key and kept the original for himself," she spats out.

"How many keys are there? I mean, Brad was killed inside, and someone had to unlock the door for that to happen."

"I don't know. At the closing, the committee was given two sets. I will ask for permission to change the locks to keys that cannot be duplicated without our knowledge. Hopefully then we can keep control of the distribution of them."

Eva and Karen set off to finish painting, and I head for the courtyard and inspect the fountain. A few hours later, Karen joins me outside. "The fountain is working beautifully."

"Yeah, I ended up taking it apart, cleaning the pieces, and fixing a small leak in the pipe. It seems to be working just fine now."

Karen grabs my face and kisses it all over. "Thank you, thank you, thank you."

I laugh. "You're welcome."

A few minutes later, Lad, Brad's nephew, walks up to me. "I got the cabinets. Want me to bring them in?"

"Sure, and I'll help you unload them." I say. Eva steps outside as well. Between the four of us, it only takes a few minutes to carry them into the kitchen.

Karen rests her hand on his arm. "We are so sorry for your loss. Your uncle was a brilliant carpenter. All of his woodworking is going to be an amazing part of this place."

Lad nods his head. "Yeah, Uncle Brad got totally Zimmerman'd. That's so wrong, but he did a righteous job with these cabinets."

"Is there anything we can do to help you?" Eva asks.

"Nah, this is Unc's dream. I'm more of a musician. I'm goin' back to the States. I got a buddy puttin' together a band. Adiós, all." Lad waves as he wanders back to his truck. I follow him as far as the garden. Curiouser and curiouser. He's willing to leave without knowing who viciously killed his uncle? What about the shop, his uncle's estate, and who'll take over the business, if anyone? I need to ask Army if he can actually leave the country.

I feel a hand on my back and jump. Karen says, "You okay? Eva and I are done inside. She's putting a few things away, then we can leave, if you're ready."

"Yup, I'm ready when you guys are."

Eva joins us in the courtyard, and we head home for the evening. Army's truck is in the driveway. When we enter the house, he's sitting at the table with his head in his hands, and when he looks up, his face is pale and tired. "¡Hola, amigos! Did you finish everything you hoped to?"

"Yes, but I had another argument with Alejo, who let himself in again and is making design decisions not approved by the Preservation Committee. He makes me so angry," Eva snaps. "I'll be glad when the project is complete."

"Eva, please remember the good he did by paying for the roof. That would have ruined your budget for the rest of the project," Army comments.

Her eyes flash with anger, but she doesn't say anything.

"Hey, Army, you get all your paperwork finished?" I ask, diverting his attention.

"Sí. It is the part of the job I dislike doing but need to do. I did secure a warrant to search Emilio's outbuilding. We can execute it tomorrow."

Smiling, I ask, "Does he know?"

"Not yet. Hopefully he won't until after we finish. I do not need him interfering or having the opportunity to eliminate any remaining evidence."

A knock at the front door catches our attention. Army opens the door and greets Victor.

"¡Buenas noches, familia! Eva, I wanted you to know that I dropped off the paint for the exterior of the hacienda. It is inside for whenever you are ready to start."

Eva's jaw drops, then tightens. "How did you get in?"

Victor's bewildered eyes dart between each of us. "I have a key."

"Where did you get it from? Alejo?" Eva asks.

"No, I have had a key for a long time. I would check on Señor Bonilla when I could."

Eva closes her eyes and sighs. "Does everyone in town have a key?"

Victor shrugs.

"How did you know what color the exterior is?" Karen asks.

"Marcyellene asked that I stop over at her house today. As part of the committee, she is aware of the approved color. She paid for everything and asked that I deliver the paint and supplies. Hopefully it is enough."

"But I am sure she cannot be bothered to come and help," Eva snaps. "Where is the paint from? I have not given the order to Juan yet."

"I picked it up in Guadalajara, not Juan's store," Victor responds.

Eva emits a low growl. "That woman! The idea for the project was to use local suppliers and materials whenever possible. There is no reason to go anywhere else. Juan was counting on that order."

"I am sorry. I did not know that. Marcyellene asked for a favor, and I was willing to help. The paint is nonreturnable."

"I am sure she did ask you for a favor," Eva says as she rubs her forehead.

Victor backs toward the door. "I am sorry to cause you a problem."

Eva places her hand on her heart. "I am sorry that I snapped at you. This is not your fault." Turning her eyes to Army, she adds, "I will need to let Juan know about this. He will be very disappointed."

Army nods in agreement. Victor lets himself out the front door.

"I am going across the street to talk to Juan," Eva says heavily.

"I'll go with you, Eva." Karen says.

"Me, too," I add.

"We will all go," Army asserts.

Once we're all in Juan's house, Eva starts, "I am sorry, Juan, but I will not be placing the order for the exterior paint for the hacienda."

He knit his eyebrows together. "Why not?"

"The paint has already been paid for and delivered," Eva replies.

"By who?"

Releasing a sigh, she says, "Marcyellene."

Juan clenches his fists. "*That* woman is not a native. She is an American." His eyes shoot daggers at Karen and me before continuing, "She just happens to live here. What is wrong with the Preservation Committee? They give work and money to outsiders. First, that woodworker, Brad, and then this. I could have ordered all the cabinets that were needed. I am not sorry he is dead."

My ears perk up. Does Juan have a motive for wanting Brad dead?

Hanging her head, Eva nods. "I am sorry. Brad is . . . was the only custom cabinet builder in town, but I wanted you to order the paint. Marcyellene's actions were done without my knowledge."

"The problem with this project is that it continues to oppress us, the *real* natives. First, the rich Spaniards invade and take everything away. Now this. I was looking forward to that order for my business."

Her face reflects great sadness. "I am sorry, Juan. I know this meant a great deal to you."

"If there is nothing else, you can leave." His eyes flare with anger.

The four of us head back across the street. Once inside, Karen hugs Eva. "I'm sorry this is so stressful. I was hoping it would be more enjoyable for you."

"Thank you. It just seems that we have too many bosses and not enough workers. I am tired and going to bed. Buenas noches."

"Buenas noches," we reply. I hug Karen, sad that there is nothing I can say to make her feel better about the situation.

"Dan, I'm gonna go to bed, too. I want this day to be over."

Army and I look at each other and shrug. There is nothing to say. We call it a night.

CHAPTER 18

The next morning, I step into the kitchen. Army looks up. "We will go to serve the warrant on Emilio's building this morning."

"But we collected the evidence the night Eva and Karen found the blood."

"Technically yes, but Emilio asked us to leave. We were not positive a crime had been committed. We will go there and notify him that we have gathered evidence. He does not need to know *when* we did that," Army replies with a broad smile. "Today I will officially place everything into evidence."

"I love it." I smile back. We each grab a cup of coffee and head for the old sugar mill. Once there, we enter the building, bagging anything we missed. The deep claw marks on the walls and floor are very disturbing. Something was very angry. Was an animal trapped inside, or is someone setting a scene to mislead us?

"Army do you know of any three-clawed animal native to this area?" I ask.

Army shakes his head slowly. "No . . . unless you consider the Chup . . . No, nothing I can think of."

I burst out a gut laugh. "You were gonna say 'Chupacabra.'"

"Fine! I was. Call it a temporary lapse in judgment. But there are no *real* animals that I can think of."

"So, I think that deep down you believe it exists. Are we adding the Chupacabra to our list of possible suspects?"

Army narrows his eyes. "You know there are places in México where your body would *never* be discovered."

I laugh. Since we had most of the evidence collected the other night, we're just finishing our final sweep of the building when Emilio appears. "What do you think you're doing?"

Army moves closer and lowers his voice. "Collecting evidence in a possible crime," he says as he hands Emilio the warrant.

Emilio's face is so red. He spits back, "I have already told you there is *NO* crime here."

Army lets a slow, sly smile cross his lips. "I hope the evidence proves you right. Adiós. Dan, we are done here." We turn and walk back to the truck.

I whisper to Army, "You don't think he'll pop a blood vessel after we leave, do you?"

"Time will tell," he replies. "After we secure this evidence, let us take our wives to lunch." As he starts the Blazer, his phone rings. "Sí. Muy bien. Gracias. Sí." Ending the call, Army has a big smile.

"Who was that?" I ask anxiously.

"Amigo, we may have a break in the Ana María Mendoza crash. A truck driver was picked up for a violation in Rio Norte and told the officers that he has some information that he will only tell me."

"How far is Rio Norte?"

"About an hour. Unfortunately, we cannot take the wives to lunch."

I slap Army on the back. "I won't tell 'em if you don't. ¡Vámonos!" We head to the station, log and secure the evidence, then travel to Rio Norte.

Once we're driving, I ask, "You said he was a truck driver. Did the local authorities impound his rig?"

"That will be one of my questions when we arrive," Army states.

"Do think this guy could also be the guy driving the cattle rustling truck? The one with the cut tire?"

"I am not sure, but if the truck is there, then we will check out the tires." He smiles. "We do not need the cast since I have the pictures on my phone yet. If there looks to be a match, then we can make a cast today and compare it to the one we have. I still have plaster in the back."

"That's a brilliant idea. Are you sure there are enough charges to hold this guy and the truck?"

Army shrugs. "I will know more once we arrive. One can hope that it will all work out."

I mull over scenarios in my mind. Could this be the thread we're looking for, that will tie some of the open cases together?

When we arrive at the Rio Norte police station, Army exchanges introductions with the officer there. I catch the gist of what is being said. The officer leads us to the back to the cell where the driver is being held. He's approximately thirty years old, rail thin, with sharp angular features, messy blond hair, and eyes the color of a fawn. I'm only catching words here and there while the driver and Army are talking. The Spanish is too fast for me.

Army looks at me. "This is Mateo Pérez. He is telling me that he received a text message asking him to arrange the accident that killed Ana María and wants to exchange it for consideration on his current charges." Mateo nods and shows Army his phone. "It has a description of José Luis' car, his license plate number, as well as where and when he would be traveling. It looks as if he was promised $10,000 for the job."

"Who's the text from?" I ask.

"José Luis."

My mouth pops open. "What?" He had his wife killed for her money, to get her out of his life, or both?

Army shrugs. "Mateo says he only got paid $2,000. He is being held here on another charge, but I am taking his phone. We need to have another discussion with José Luis." Army and I shake hands with the officer and thank them. The truck Mateo was driving was impounded for equipment violations. We make our way around the vehicle, checking each tire, but they don't have a cut in any of them. Army asks that it also be processed for fingerprints and DNA to find out who else has been in the cab. We're hoping to get lucky.

We head back to town and find Valeria sitting in the doorframe of the station with her back against the locked door. She struggles to get to her feet. Army approaches, and she starts to cry. I don't understand what she's saying between her rapidly spoken Spanish and her sobbing. Army nods continuously as he opens the door and helps her to a chair. It breaks my heart to see her so sad. I bring her a bottle of water.

"Sí, sí, gracias," Army says, then turns to me. "It appears that we have something else to speak to José Luis about. Valeria is saying that he is the father of her baby, but he refuses to marry her. Her father threw her out of his house. She is staying with her tía for now."

Rubbing my forehead, all I can think is that this looks very bad for José Luis.

"We will drive her back to her tía's house, then pay a call on José Luis."

I nod in agreement.

Valeria stands up, then doubles over. Her jeans are soaked down both legs. *Oh, her water broke.* She starts to yell in Spanish. I understand the tone and the word 'momma.' Army and I exchange glances.

"Give me your phone. I'll call an ambulance," I offer.

"No time. She says the baby is coming now!" Army replies. Valeria is holding her stomach and screaming.

"Not now. First babies take forever. We can wait for the EMTs."

Army snaps, "Not according to the one who is pregnant. Let's get her back in the truck and to the clinic. It will be faster than waiting for the ambulance."

Half lifting, half pushing, we finally get her in the back seat. I sit next to her and grab her hand, telling her that everything's going to be fine and we'll be at the hospital soon. Army drops the Trailblazer in gear and floors it. Valeria's crying and crushing my hand, Army's eyes are focused on the road, and all I can think is that it feels like slow motion. I imitate the breathing techniques Karen and I learned when she was pregnant. She's not listening. She is rocking back and forth, crying.

At the clinic, Army slams the truck into 'Park' and runs full-out through the front doors. He returns with a gurney pushed by the nurse practitioner and another staff member. Together, we help Valeria out and onto the cart. She is crying and speaking Spanish.

"What is she saying?" I ask.

"She wants her mom," Army states, following everyone into the clinic. "We can call her tía and let her know what is happening. She can call the mom."

"Phew, I'm way too old for this stuff." I'm laughing, and so is he. He calls the aunt, and within a few minutes, she arrives at the clinic. She uses her finger to tap Army's chest while talking. He nods patiently. I stand off to the side until she is finished.

Once back in the Trailblazer, Army says, "Her tía is going to demand that José Luis take a paternity test."

"Will he?"

"If the courts force it, but I will wait for the court order before I bring that up. We will talk with José Luis regarding what we have learned about the accident."

His house is a sprawling, two-story mansion. A maid answers the door. She asks us to wait in the hall while she speaks to José Luis. He appears a few minutes later, dressed in a casual two-piece suit and black sandals. "¿Cómo está, Comisario? What can I do for you?"

"We have some new evidence in the accident that killed your wife and would like to talk to you about it."

His face lights up. "Really? Please, come and sit down."

We are shown to a formal living room. Army and José Luis sit across from each other on duplicate white couches. I choose a chair to the side of them. *Very 1970's swinger pad. I'm amazed they aren't fur-covered.* "Now, what is this new evidence?" José asks, leaning forward.

On the edge of the sofa, Army also leans forward. "Well, a witness has come forward with a claim that it was not an accident that caused Ana María's death. There appears to be some validity to the information."

José Luis sits bolt upright. "Who is this person? What evidence suggests it is not an accident? He is lying."

"How do you know it is a 'he'?" Army asks.

"I am using 'he' in general. He *or* she is lying," he snaps.

Army quietly asks, "Why do you think the person is lying? José Luis, may I see your phone?"

He hands it to Army, who questions, "This looks new. Would you have a second phone?"

José Luis shrugs. "No. I had another phone, but it fell out of my pocket and was too damaged to use, so I bought a new one."

Army's eyes flick with skepticism. "That's a shame. Did you keep the same number?"

"No" comes the response.

"Would I be able to get the number from someone in the family or the name of the carrier?"

José Luis again just shrugs.

Army stands and extends his hand. "Thank you for your time. We will be in touch." I nod to José Luis.

Once in the truck, I slap Army's shoulder. "You're gonna subpoena his phone records, right?"

"Absolutely, and check public records. He was more concerned that someone was lying than the fact that his wife's death may not have been an accident."

"Yeah, he didn't seem interested in any details. He was defensive." *My coppy sense is telling me there is something there. He has a new phone and is making accusations that the witness is lying?*

Army drums his fingers on the steering wheel. "What are you thinking?" I ask.

"If he is liquidating his wife's estate, I want to know, and to whom he is selling. I need to follow the money."

"I wish I could help more, but my Spanish isn't strong enough to read documents or help write the subpoena."

"Thank you, amigo, but this is something I need to do. We should get home and check with Karen and Eva if there's anything you can help with at the hacienda. Anything that I do not need to do helps me."

I nod in agreement but want in on the next step of the case.

"Hopefully soon I will be able to get the evidence from the outbuilding to the crime lab. You want to come?"

"Sure. The results from the other stuff we brought in should be ready."

"Good." Army puts the truck in gear and heads for home.

Walking into the kitchen, I notice it's suppertime, and Army and I haven't eaten all day. Eva soon has beef tacos with all the sides. Sitting at the table, I ask Eva about projects that still need to be done at the hacienda.

"The plaster was repaired today and will need time to dry, then that wall will need to be painted, *again,*" she states.

"Again?" I ask.

Eva rolls her eyes. "When Alejo pulled his picture down, the wire caught and tore one of the metal eye hooks out of the wall. It left a hole, and we had to have the wall repaired a second time." She holds up a set of keys and shakes them. "Luckily, the Preservation Committee approved changing the locks. Victor did it today. Now there are only three sets. I have one, the Committee Chairperson has one, and Marcyellene will have one."

"I still don't think it is a good idea for her to have a set. I don't trust her," Karen says.

"I agree with you, but that was the decision of the committee. I will just have to live with it," Eva replies. "I will drop it off to her tomorrow."

Army holds up his hands. "Can we not discuss the politics of the situation now? I think it is a good time for us to settle into a game of *Clue*. I bet I find the murderer."

My eyes flick to Karen. I never count her out when it comes to solving a murder case.

"We accept your challenge, mi esposo." Eva laughs.

Dinner finished, we step into the living room when Army's phone rings. He moves back into the kitchen, then joins us again and announces that the call was from Valeria's aunt, and she had a healthy baby boy. Both mother and baby are fine. No name for the baby, yet. The rest of the evening is filled with laughter and good-natured verbal jabs as to each other's investigator skills.

CHAPTER 19

The next morning, Karen and I accompany Eva to give Marcyellene a key to the hacienda and have the uncomfortable conversation about the paint order.

"It's about a mile walk, if you don't mind," Eva states.

"Of course," says Karen. "We're right behind you."

Marcyellene's house is a modern take on the traditional Mexican home: two stories painted a warm beige with a large second-floor balcony. It's set back from the roadway, with red ceramic roof tiles and intricate wrought iron screens over each window. Blue stone tiles cover the stairs to the impressive double wooden front door. An expansive lawn and manicured flower beds are impressive. *I wonder how much of the town's water is needed to maintain this landscape?*

Ernesto stands in a flower bed, chomping on something that used to be flowers. I snicker at his total irreverence. He appears less than impressed by our arrival and bites off another mouthful as we pass by. We are approaching the stairs leading to the house when the front door swings open wildly. Marcyellene appears on the porch with a large butcher knife in her hand, then runs down the stairs, screaming, "Get off my property! I told you before if I ever catch you here, I'll kill you!"

Karen and Eva just stop. I step in front of them both.

"What the . . ." Karen stutters.

As Marcyellene runs at us, I step to the side, sticking my foot out to trip her. She makes contact, falls, and lands facedown in the grass. I step on her wrist until she releases the knife, then I pick it up.

"What are you doing, asshole?" she spits out, rolling onto her back.

"I wasn't about to let you attack us," I snap, looking down at her.

Marcyellene gets to her feet without any help from my extended hand. "I wasn't attacking you, idiot. It's that goat. I hate him! He's ruined every flower bed I have. I swear he's some form of a demon."

I bite the inside of my lip to stop from laughing. "He's a goat. That's what they do. Have you tried putting fencing around the beds?"

"Why didn't I think of that? Oh, wait, I have. He stands on the fencing and seems to be able to get past anything I put up."

"Threatening Ernesto with a knife seems extreme."

"Well, I don't have a gun, and I'm at the end of my rope," Marcyellene replies nonchalantly as she dusts off her pants. "I have a position to uphold. My home and gardens are the highlight of the village. I've even had Victor string electric wire on the property line, hoping it'll scare him off or make him decapitate himself."

Karen gasps in horror. "That's a terrible thing to do. Not only to a goat, but what if there were children running around? They could be seriously hurt or killed."

Marcyellene shrugs. "I have no children of my own, and at my age, there aren't going to be any, so none should be running around my property."

Karen and Eva stand with their mouths gaping.

Marcyellene narrows her eyes. "Why are you here?"

Eva clears her throat, but before she can say anything, Marcyellene pushes past her. "UGGGHHH, he's still eating my flowers. Get him out!" She looks at me as she points to Ernesto.

He paws at the ground, puts his nose in the dirt, and comes up with something in his mouth. I walk over to him, and he drops the item. I reach to pick it up, but stop and take a closer look. "Eva, could you call Army, please? Let him know we may have discovered possible evidence."

Eva nods and pulls out her cell phone.

Karen moves next to me. "What is it?"

"It looks like a homemade three-clawed item. Something that could have been used to kill Juan Mercado and Brad."

Marcyellene leans toward it.

"Don't touch it," I say far louder than I wanted.

Her head snaps up. "It's not mine. I don't know how it got here."

"Everyone back up. This is possible evidence," I say. "Army will need to collect it and have it processed."

Everyone steps back onto the walkway. Ernesto finishes his mouthful of food, burps, and saunters off. His tail twitches as he walks away.

"If you find out that the goat did it, does it get a death sentence? I'm thinking a nice stew with him as the main ingredient," Marcyellene says sarcastically. "I'll be inside when the Comisario shows up." She turns and stomps up the porch stairs.

Eva calls after her, "We stopped over to discuss some issues with the hacienda. Can we come inside and talk?"

Marcyellene stops mid-step, turns, and plants her feet. "You people don't understand how busy I am. I don't have time for petty complaints. You're welcome for the paint, but I must get ready to go. I have a meeting in town. If the Comisario doesn't get here soon, he'll miss me completely." She continues into the house, slamming the front door behind her.

"That went well," Karen snaps. We are left to stand on the sidewalk until Army arrives several minutes later.

He gets out of the truck and throws up his hands. "What? I cannot leave you three alone?" He grins.

I laugh. "Well, you're gonna need gloves and evidence bags."

Army moves to the back of the Trailblazer, then joins me at the flower bed as he pulls on gloves and leans down to pick up the claw. A low whistle escapes his lips. "This looks dangerous. Someone went to a great deal of trouble to make this."

"Is there blood on the tips?" I ask.

"Could be. It is hard to see with the dirt on it. I will let the lab examine it and make the determination. How did it get here, and why?"

Everyone shrugs.

"I will bag and tag it, along with the surrounding soil. Dan, can you photograph it first? I will also need to speak to Marcyellene." Army rolls his eyes. "Eva, you and Karen can head home. This may take some time. I'll take your statements later." They nod and walk away.

Army and I process the scene. When we're done, Army jerks his head in the direction of the front door. "Let's do this."

We knock. When Marcyellene answers, she's wearing a different top. This one is extremely low-cut. Cooing, she says, "Comisario, how good it is to see you, again. Please, come in."

"Thank you," Army replies with complete calm. "What can you tell me about the item found in your front yard?"

"I don't know anything about it. Obviously, someone, excuse the pun, planted it there. If I thought it was possible, I'd say the damn goat did it," she answers with a dramatic sigh.

"Did you notice anything in any of your other flower beds when you were working on them?"

"Pfft, I have a professional gardener. These hands were not made for manual labor." She holds up ten immaculately manicured fingernails. *I don't have a lot of sympathy for her. Would it be wrong to start hoping she's the killer? I doubt she is though.*

"I will need the name of your gardener. Has anyone suspicious been in the neighborhood? Anything or anyone you can think of?"

"His name is Ruben Herrera, and he has not brought anything to my attention. Sorry, I must dash. I'm the guest speaker at a ladies' luncheon."

Army bows his head. "I will need you to come to the station and make a formal statement."

A wicked smile creases her lips. "You call, I'll come."

"What about tomorrow at 10:00 a.m. at my office?" Army asks.

She winks. "That works."

"Thank you for your cooperation. We can see ourselves to the door."

"The pleasure was all mine," she replies as she closes the door behind us.

Once back in the truck, Army and I laugh and shake our heads.

"Mi amigo, after I log these things into evidence, let's go home."

When we arrive at the station, Army quickly records everything into evidence and secures it. He makes a call to Ruben Herrera, who confirms that there was nothing in any of Marcyellene's flower beds when he was there two days ago. He weeded all of her gardens.

"We can head home for lunch," Army says.

Karen and Eva are at the kitchen table. Army interviews each separately.

"You all reported the same thing," he says after the interviews are done. "Ernesto was there when you arrived. You were focused on Marcyellene's actions when the item was discovered, and no one at the scene touched it until I secured it. I will have your statements typed and ready for signature tomorrow. I need to take the new evidence to Guadalajara this afternoon."

"I'll go with you," I say. Army nods.

"That is fine, mi esposo," Eva replies. "The plants for the hacienda have arrived, and Karen, Sara, and I are going to start planting things in the courtyard."

"If you need help, Dan and I can do it when we get back."

After lunch, Army and I head out to the truck with Karen following us. "Dan, can I speak to you, please?"

I step toward the back of the Trailblazer. "What did I do?" I ask.

Karen laughs. "Nothing yet. It's what I'd like you to do."

"What?"

"I think we need to ask everyone out for dinner. This case is getting more complicated, and I think we should step away from it for an evening."

"You know I hate to stop while in an investigation," I say.

"I know, and I love your determination, but these people are also our friends. Let's have a little fun, please."

I shift from foot to foot.

Karen continues, "I also think we're gonna be tired after planting."

I do hate to stop the investigation, but I owe Karen some time. This is a vacation. "Okay, I'll talk to Army," I agree.

"Thank you, mi esposo," Karen whispers as she kisses me goodbye.

"Is everything okay?" Army asks when I climb into the truck.

"Yes, Karen wants us all to go out for dinner. She thinks everyone will be tired after today, and I agree with the idea. Our treat after everything you guys have done for us."

Army nods but is quiet on the way to the station to pick up the evidence and later on the drive to the crime lab. I appreciate the need to review the pieces of the puzzle until a picture emerges. I sit back and study the 'claw.'

It looks like something familiar that has been reconfigured. Three metal sharpened prongs, spaced equally apart, wrapped in what appears to be plaster and soaked gauze, and painted black. I can hardly wait for the lab to give us specifics.

CHAPTER 20

We step into the front entrance of the lab. Dr. Luis Rodriguez is walking down the hall. "¡Hola, amigos! Please tell me you do not have another dead body."

Army sighs. "Luckily no, but I do have more work for the lab. Do you think this could have made the marks on my two victims' necks?" He shows the claw to Luis.

Luis takes the evidence bag and rotates it to look at the weapon from various angles, then nods his head several times. "Yes, yes. This may have done it. The lab will get specifics so I can be sure. Where did you find it?"

"An unofficial aide unearthed it," Army replies with a broad smile.

Luis knits his eyebrows together but doesn't ask any questions. We shake hands farewell and exit the lab. The evidence turned in, Army says, "Let's get home and see if Eva and Karen need help."

While we drive back, I say, "I think Karen's idea of going out is a good one. A few drinks and a nice meal will be fun. What do ya think?"

"If you wish," he replies quietly.

Army seems to have something on his mind. Does he know something I don't? "You all right?" I inquire.

"I am tired. Tired of looking at people I know, wondering if they have done these terrible things. I want this to be solved."

"I'm sorry, my friend. I know we will solve it," I reply.

"But when?"

I shrug a response.

Army rubs his fingers on his temples. "I am sorry, too. This is not your problem. Please, let us go out tonight with our beautiful wives."

When Army and I enter the courtyard at the hacienda, I stop to take it all in. The transformation is amazing. Electric pink bougainvillea are on the walls, while in the beds beneath, dwarf palms and pink desert roses stand tall. The restored fountain is a central focal point, burbling a soothing rhythm, surrounded by a raised bed interspersed with green agave and brilliant orange bird of paradise plants. Colored pots of varying sizes hold lady slippers, marigolds, and blue dahlias. The main door is flanked on both sides by purple gladiolus. Sage used as ground cover fills the air with a sweet, minty smell.

Eva is planting near the fountain. Looking up, she says, "¡Hola! I am glad to see you back."

"Eva, this is beautiful. The place looks like it's coming back to life," I declare with a broad smile.

"Well then, thank your wife. She is a genius with plants. All her research and hard work have paid off."

"Speaking of my wife, where is she?"

"I'm right behind you, Dan." Karen laughs.

I spin around. "I know you picked each plant for its symbolism. Can you tell me what they are?"

Karen smiles. "All the plants have a connection to Mexico and are used to vary height and keep the visitor's eyes moving around the garden. Dahlias are the national flower of Mexico, and blue symbolizes a fresh start and big changes. Marigolds, or cempasúchil, reflect the fragility of life. Gladiolus represent sympathy and memories. They were given to victorious warriors because their shape resembles a sword."

"I enjoy the agave because we are in Jalisco, where tequila is made," I add.

"Why am I not surprised," Karen snickers.

"Marigolds are used for Día de los Muertos, correct?"

"Yes."

"It is amazing," I say. Looking at Karen, I notice a streak of dirt on her right cheek, mud on her shirt, and pink and white gardening gloves on her hands, and she's holding a small metal tool. "What's that?"

Karen looks at her hands. "My gloves?"

"No, I know what gloves are. That metal tool. Can I see it?" I ask. She hands it to me, and I turn it over and over. "Army, look at this. Could something like this have been modified to the claw we found? A garden cultivator?"

He studies it. "I think it could be. Hopefully, the crime lab will determine if it is and come up with a brand. The only problem is if it is common, we would not have a way to narrow down who bought the one we have. Also, all of your statements will be ready for your signature tomorrow."

We all nod.

"When the lab has the results, we can start looking at home improvement and garden stores," I say.

Karen leans into me and whispers, "You understand that Juan has a home improvement store here in town."

I shoot Karen an 'I know' look, and I'm uneasy to mention it to Army, but do. "I'm sorry. I don't mean to imply . . ."

Army holds up his hand. "I know. I must do this job right, even if I need to investigate family. I will wait to see what the lab finds out."

Victor unexpectedly enters the courtyard. He stops, then crosses his arms over his chest as he surveys the garden. He looks at Eva and grins. "This is very beautiful."

Eva sighs. "Thank you. It just makes me a little sad that neither Ana María or Brad will see it completed."

Karen nods in agreement. "I think they both would have been pleased with the progress so far."

"Do you still have a lot to do?" I ask.

"We need to install the kitchen cabinets, paint the exterior, finish the landscaping, and then stage it for the grand opening. I am nervous that things will not be done in time," Eva admits.

"I can be here all day tomorrow," I reply. I can't believe I'm taking myself out of the investigation, but I want Eva and Karen to be successful in this endeavor.

"Muchas gracias, Dan," Eva states.

Victor adds, "Sara has asked that I help, too."

Eva releases a deep breath. "Then the only big project left is painting the exterior. I will be happy when this is done."

"I cannot help tomorrow, but the day after I hope to," Army says.

"Thank you, mi amor. I will see who else can help that day. Karen, we will need to make sure we have enough supplies. I can call Juan tonight to see if we can pick up things from his store tomorrow."

"If everyone is ready, let's call it a day and head for dinner," I say. "The Hotel del Sol is having a jazz band tonight. It could be fun."

We head home and clean up. An hour or so later, the four of us are sitting at a table in the Hotel del Sol, drinks in hand with Juan and Carlota, who were already there when we arrived. Victor and Sara join us.

Eva asks Juan about the painting supplies. He confirms that he has everything in stock. Sarcastically, he asks, "Are you sure that Marcyellene does not want to order those things for you from Guadalajara?"

Eva places her hand on the table near Juan. "Again, I am sorry about the paint. Can we please work together?"

Juan presses a tight smile on his lips and nods. Eva asks people at the table about their availability to help paint.

Once we get our drinks, I pick up my glass. "Here's to a successful end to the hacienda restoration." Everyone clinks glasses. Various conversations start until the food arrives, and we tuck into our dinners. The band begins playing, and another round of drinks is ordered. The evening is relaxed and laughter-filled. We walk home, saying good night to Victor and Sara as we leave, then later to Juan and Carlota, who make their way across the street. I'm happy that Eva and Juan are friendly again.

Once inside the house, Army pulls me aside. "I have a message that the lab has the results on the claw."

"Already? That was fast. What did it say?" I ask.

Army smiles. "Luis asked the lab to make it a priority. He also has all the information from Brad's autopsy. I will go tomorrow and pick up everything."

I sigh heavily. "I can't go. I promised to help at the hacienda."

"I know. I will bring it all home. We can sit here and discuss theories in private."

"Isn't Marcyellene coming in to sign her statement tomorrow at 10:00 a.m.?"

Army throws his head back. "UGGGGHHHH. I forgot about that. I guess I will do that first, then head to Guadalajara."

I put my hand over my mouth to hide my snickering. Army's eyes narrow, then he too is laughing.

"Just have Diego meet with Marcyellene."

"I would fear for the boy's safety. I think she is a maneater." Army shakes his head. "No, I am Comisario. I will handle it."

"Stay safe." I laugh, then add, "Did Luis say anything about finding fingerprints or DNA?"

"He left me a message that he had results. I called back, but got his voicemail. I left a message."

I step into the bedroom where we have all the evidence. My eyes travel from one scene to another.

Army stands next to me. "What are you thinking, my friend?"

"It's here. One thing will open this investigation up. We need one fingerprint or piece of DNA."

"*And* we need to have someone to compare it to," he adds.

"True." I start to form an idea, but how do I approach Army with it? It's a bit devious and would involve family members.

"Mi amigo, I can see the wheels of your mind working. What are you thinking?"

"I'm thinking about how we solved the murders in Ireland. The problem is, this is also your family."

Army nods. "Tell me, and I will decide if it is something I am willing to do."

"On that vacation, once the DNA was discovered at the crime scene, Karen and I hosted a party. The local cop bagged and tagged used glasses from all the guests. The glasses were then processed for fingerprints and DNA." I look at Army sheepishly.

He shifts from side to side. "I will need time to think on this. First, the lab needs to determine if there are any fingerprints or DNA on the claw. If there is, then I will decide about your idea, but . . . this is *my* family."

Is he concerned that his family is involved? What was I thinking putting him in this situation? "I'm sorry I suggested it. I don't mean to make this more difficult for you."

"Do not feel bad. Someone has done terrible things and needs to be stopped. The good news is that the samples could clear everyone in the family," Army replies with a broad smile. "We will wait for the results."

He heads toward his bedroom, then stops and faces me. "I have DNA evidence that can be compared."

"You do? Where?" I ask.

"Me," he replies.

I knit my brows together. "Oh . . . okay. Is this a confession that you did all these horrible things?"

Army laughs. "No, amigo. I have blood that can be submitted for DNA testing."

"Your DNA can rule in or out a familial match. Are you sure you want to do this?"

"Sí. If it rules out my family, I will feel better moving forward with the investigation."

I hesitate. "What if it rules someone in?"

Army holds up his hand. "I will do what is needed. I will ask for a blood draw tomorrow when I am at the lab." His face looks more relaxed, and he stands as if a weight has been lifted. "Good night, my friend. Sleep well."

I must trust my friend to do what is right, even if it involves family, but what if . . .

CHAPTER 21

The next morning, Karen and I are up early, dressed, caffeinated, and at the hacienda. Victor arrives with his tools, and Eva directs cabinet placement. After several centuries, nothing in the room is square or level. I think Victor is swearing under his breath, but with it being in Spanish, it's hard to tell.

"Eva, I am out of shims for the cabinets," Victor states. "I'll go to Juan's store and get some. I will be back soon."

The minute that Victor walks out the door, a singsongy voice calls out, "¡Hola!"

Eva rolls her eyes. "That is all I need. Alejo."

"There you are!" Alejo appears in the kitchen. His musky cologne descends upon us and makes my eyes water. "You have not been open to my decorating ideas, but you will approve of this mirror I have. It is an original period piece from my father-in-law's grandmother's home in Spain. I have the perfect spot for it." He turns on his heels and heads for the living room without waiting for a response.

Eva emits a low growl.

We follow him. Karen is cleaning in the room when he appears. She makes eye contact with me, a look of confusion on her face. I shrug.

Alejo saunters to the far wall of the living room. "Here on the wall. It will reflect everything and make the room seem twice as big," he announces.

It is a beautiful mirror. Iron scrollwork frames the top and bottom, and it's covered in a mosaic of tiles in rich orange, deep blue, buttery yellow, and black. It appears aged and appropriate for the house, but I'm not a designer.

Eva rubs both of her temples. Karen jumps in, "That's a magnificent mirror. Thank you. I'm sure we can find a place for it."

Alejo turns, speaking slowly and deliberately. "*No!* I will be hanging it. Hold this." He hands the mirror to Karen. She looks at it, then him. "Picture wire wasn't used in the 1800s."

He stares back at her. "No one will see it." He pulls a hammer from his pocket and proceeds to pound a nail into the restored plaster wall. Eva holds her chest as if the nail is being driven into her instead of the wall. He lifts the mirror into place, then steps back to admire his work. "Perfect. I must leave. Adiós."

Karen calls after him, "We're painting the exterior tomorrow and could use your help!"

He calls back, never breaking stride out the door, "I have told you before, I do not paint!"

"Of course, you don't," Karen mutters. "Eva, do you want me to leave the mirror where it is?"

Eva throws her hands up. "Yes, for now." I assist Karen with cleaning the room. We work in silence, stunned and angry by Alejo's visit, until Victor returns. He and I get back to work on the cabinets. Several hours into the day, the kitchen is pulled together. I stop and think about Brad and the senselessness of his death. What a waste. He could have been very proud of his work. I continue to review the evidence of his murder in my mind. One missing piece will solve it, but what is it?

Eva stops in. "This looks amazing. Thank you both, but it is time for a break. Let's go home for lunch. I have leftovers we can eat."

We're sitting around the kitchen table when Army arrives with a stack of papers. He motions for me to follow him into the evidence room. "I stopped at the courthouse and went through Ana María's legal paperwork. José Luis inherited her estate, of course. What's interesting is that the day after her funeral, Emilio filed to act as José Luis' financial agent of all the accounts."

"Really? Filing as a financial agent, do you think they were in this together?" I ask.

"I am not sure. I want to compare José's signature to other documents. His phone records for both his home and mobile are in. I still need to review them."

Army also goes over the information from the crime lab. A human fingerprint *and* DNA were found, as well as goat DNA, but there was no match to anyone.

"Well, it's good that it's not your direct family member, but disappointing that we didn't find someone. We need to think of a way to legally collect other's DNA."

"I spoke to Eva about your idea of a party to collect samples. She understands that we need to catch this person, or persons, but she will not deceive anyone."

I nod in agreement. "I can appreciate that. And I can help with the phone records."

We sit with the pages of phone records, looking for any messages between José Luis and the truck driver, Mateo.

"I can only find one call between them. It's on the day of the crash from José's cell about an hour before it happened," I say.

"That doesn't make sense. If this was done to kill his wife, how did they arrange it?" Army asks. "I doubt they would risk meeting in person. Did he have another phone, or did he use someone else's phone?"

"If Emilio has control of the estate, maybe they're in it together. He may have set everything up, then on that day, all José needed to do was confirm the location and time. Could you get Emilio's phone records?"

"I requested them shortly after José's. I hope they will be here soon," Army replies as a sly grin creeps across his face.

"Maybe it's time to have another talk with José. Either get his reaction to this news or see if he lies to us," I say.

"It is as if you can read my mind. I asked him and Emilio in for an interview tomorrow morning."

"They're not family, right?"

Army shakes his head. "No, they are not family. Why?"

"I think if they both come in, as a courtesy, we should offer each one something to drink. When the interview is over and the beverage containers are left behind . . ."

Army finishes my sentence. "They are considered abandoned and free for us to take to process for DNA. I like it!"

Walking up to the evidence wall, he scans both names as suspects listed under the car crash, then steps back. "Even if we are able to prove they set this up, without DNA we cannot prove they were involved in any of these other crimes."

"The nature of the other crimes, they're up close, personal, and intensely violent. That's very different than hiring a third party. Why not arrange an 'accident' at home? It seems to me there are two types of mindsets at work."

"You are right. I have always suspected that there is more than one person behind these crimes. How do we find them?" Army asks.

A knock at the bedroom door interrupts us. Eva sticks her head in. "¡Hola! Karen and I would like company on a walk. Would you both join us, please?"

Army and I meet them in the living room. We step out onto the sidewalk into the cool early evening. The sky is a purplish-black color, and the stars are just barely visible. Karen and Eva quickly head back inside to grab sweaters when Army's phone buzzes in his breast pocket. "Sí, bueno?" He pauses, then repeatedly nods his head. I hope he understands that no one on the other end can see this. "Sí . . . sí . . . sí." I hear someone yelling in Spanish, then they abruptly hang up. Army winces and looks at me. "Some days it is not good to be the Comisario General."

Karen and Eva join us again. Army informs them he has had a call he needs to investigate, and they nod in acknowledgement. He states, "Dan, with me, please." We head for the truck. "Who was the caller?" I ask once we're inside.

"*That* was Valeria's mother. The paternity test came back negative for José Luis, and it ruled out Emilio since he's a close family member. Valeria is now saying that she was drinking at the Hotel del Sol bar one night, had too much, and was lured to a hotel room and sexually assaulted by someone who must be the father. She is accusing my brother-in-law, Victor." Army's eyes fill with pain.

"Oh, no! This is bad. Whaddaya gonna do?"

"I must have a discussion with him regarding these charges."

What is Valeria up to? Is she protecting the real father, or will any wealthy man do? What will this do to the family if it's true? I'm not sure I even believe Valeria at this point.

The drive to Sara and Victor's house is quiet. I have no words to help my friend with this situation. Army knocks on the front door.

Sara opens it with a smile. "¡Buenas noches! ¿Qué pasó?"

Army's face is emotionless as he asks, "Is Victor home?"

Concern fills Sara's eyes as she searches Army's face, but she moves to the side to allow us to step into the hall. Victor appears out of his office. "Buenas noches."

"Can we speak in private?" Army asks.

"Sí, adelante." Victor furrows his brow, then gestures for us to step into his office. He moves behind a large wooden desk and motions to the chairs in front of it. We sit down.

"How can I help you?" he asks, reclining in his chair.

Army leans forward. "Victor, I received a report today that implicates you in a sexual assault on a young lady."

Victor's face flushes a deep red as he sits bolt upright. "Who says this?"

"Valeria Flores," Army replies firmly.

"Do not believe her. She is a whore. I have heard she has slept with many men. Now she has a child and is looking for a man to support her. I have money."

Army's reply is slow and deliberate. "A court order will be issued for your DNA to check paternity. We need to talk to Sara."

"How can you allow this? You know me. I do not assault women," Victor snaps.

"What I do know is that while married to my sister, you have had more than one affair. Sara tolerates it, so I have said nothing about it." Army's voice is nearly a growl. "Tell me the truth, did this happen?"

Victor replies through a clenched jaw, "No! If you do not believe this of me, you can leave my home, now!"

Army stands up, his anger evident in his clenched jaw. "First, I will speak to Sara. True or not, the test will happen, and people will know you have been accused. She has a right to know."

Victor pounds his fist on the desk, stands up, and points at Army. "¡Cómo te atreves!"

I want to slap that arrogant smirk off his face. Anger flashes in Army's eyes. Army points me toward the hall. I step out, closing the door behind me, but stay near it in case he needs me. I hear Victor yelling in Spanish but can't hear clearly enough to understand.

When the door reopens, Army joins me. Victor slams the door closed behind us.

"He admit to anything?" I ask.

Army is clenching his fists. "He said the person that tried to kill me had the right. Too bad they failed. Now, I will speak with my sister, alone."

I nod. "I'll wait near the front door."

"Gracias," Army replies breathlessly.

Sara walks into the hall from the kitchen, and Army motions for her to move to the dining room. I catch words in Spanish, but not enough to understand what is said. I do hear Sara saying, "No, no," followed by crying. In my career, I've had this conversation far too often. No matter how it's said, hearing the words hurt. Several minutes pass, then Army returns to the hall. His face is drawn and pale. My heart breaks for my friend. We walk slowly toward the truck as the rain starts.

Army stops and points his face toward the sky, letting the rain fall on his face. "One good thing." We get in and head home.

CHAPTER 22

I absentmindedly stir my morning coffee while I go over the events of last night. My thoughts oscillate between sadness for this family, especially my friend at these accusations, and wanting to be sure that justice is served. Army joins me at the table.

"How's Eva doing with the news from last night?"

"She is very sad, as I am. If Valeria files a formal complaint against Victor, I will have no choice but to arrest and have him charged." He shrugs.

"I'm sorry, my friend."

"I know. Also, Emilio and José Luis will come to the station at 11:00 this morning. I told them I have new evidence in their case. I would like you there."

I nod in agreement. I'm curious what tone the meeting will take. Will Emilio be angry, José Luis defensive, or one or both lash out at Army? Suddenly, a loud bleat sounds through the kitchen window. We look up, and Jesús stares in. His face shows anxiety as he waves to us to come outside. Army shakes his head in disbelief. We step outside and find Jesús and Ernesto on the driveway waiting for us. Jesús speaks rapidly in Spanish, points to the west, then walks away. Army responds, "Sí . . . sí." He turns to me. "Jesús reports that Ernesto witnessed another herd of cattle being stolen last night from the ranch of Tomás Blanco. He told us to go investigate it. I know the place. Do you want to come with me?"

Army and I drive to the home of Señor Blanco. He confirms that eighteen of his cows were stolen after midnight. After the heavy rains in the evening, he had moved the herd to a different pasture. He checked on them around 11:00 p.m, and they were all there, but gone when he went back at 6:00 a.m. Army promises him he will make a report, investigate it, and let him know what he finds. He shakes Tomás' hand as we say goodbye.

Once we're back in the truck, Army says, "We need to go to the Smith Cattle Processing Plant. I want to see if Tomás' cows are there."

We pull into the gravel drive of the plant and park next to one of six white boarded pens that occupy an open area. The area is surprisingly quiet compared to our last visit. Few trucks and fewer people. As we step out of the Trailblazer, the smell of blood, urine, and feces overpowers my nose. The flies are incessant. Army leans over the fence of the pen filled with cows. "These are Tomás' stolen cattle. They have his brand on them."

"Army, can you see the horn of the cow closest to you?" I point it out. "Is that blood?"

A broad smile creases Army's face. "I think it is. Watch that cow while I get the evidence kit." Army picks up the kit from the back of his truck and hurries back. We look around, see no one in the area, and climb over the fence. Army easily grabs one of the cows. It pays to show up with an experienced cowboy. "Hold the head still while I swab it," he says. I try to grab the cow's neck, but it shakes free of my grasp and loudly moos.

"SHHHHH," Army snaps.

"Don't tell me, tell him or her," I say, grabbing the cow around the neck a second time. It tosses its head repeatedly.

"Hold it still."

"I'm trying. You realize I'm not the former cowboy in this situation."

"All right, all right. Give me a little room to get at the horn." I glare at Army but lean back while still holding the head.

He swabs the horn and places it in an evidence bag. "This may be our big break in the rustling ring."

I release the cow as it decides to head-bang my left side. Ouch! I'm sure that's going to leave a bruise. Army and I scramble over the fence and onto the driveway. I look down and notice tire tracks, then nudge Army. "That distinctive tire tread is here. The one with a cut in it. The gang stole Tomás' cattle."

"We need to have a talk with the manager again." Army smirks and slaps me on the back.

We make our way to the single-story brick office building. The same short, fat man is behind the desk, twisting a pen between his fingers. The pungent smell of his hair cream fills the air. Disheveled papers in towering piles cover every flat surface, spill over onto the floor, and form a circle around the desk. His two bodyguards jump from their chairs when we enter. Both look like moving solid brick walls.

"¿Cómo están, señores?" the man asks.

Army reaches his hand forward. "I am Comisario General Armando Gómez, remember? I don't believe you mentioned your name last time we met."

An annoyed look crosses the man's face as he shakes Army's hand. "Carlos Pérez. Why are you here?" He places both elbows on the desk and leans forward. Cool, or trying to play it cool.

"This is my partner, Dan Novice. We are interested in the herd of cows you have in one of your pens. When did they arrive, and who delivered them?"

Carlos waves his hand dismissively. "I am sorry. It has been busy, and I have not kept up with all the paperwork. If you leave your phone number, I will call you when I find that information." Never breaking eye contact, he leans back in his chair, pressing his fingertips together. The bodyguards snicker.

Army places both of his palms on the desk and leans in. "A name, *now,* or I will secure a warrant, shut this place down for a long, *slooow* investigation of your property, the company accounts, health department surveys, and anything else I can think of." A tight grin spreads across his lips.

Carlos shrugs and shuffles through the papers on his desk. He pulls one out. "They came in yesterday. The trucking company is Dos Hermanos. I do not remember the driver."

"Who owns it?" I ask, looking between Carlos and Army.

Carlos' eyes shift to me. "I send payment to the Conquistador Company. I do not have the name of the owner."

Army clears his throat. "Those cows will remain here and unharmed until the owner makes the proper arrangements."

Carlos gives a curt nod of acknowledgement. Army and I head back to the truck.

"Do you believe his story?" I ask.

"Yes. I do not get the feeling that he is the mastermind behind the cattle rustling." Army's phone rings, and as he answers it, I hear yelling in Spanish. He holds it away from his ear, then the call abruptly ends.

I bite my lip to stop from laughing. "I'm sorry. I shouldn't laugh, but I don't miss those kinds of calls. Who was it?"

He sighs. "That was Valeria's mother, Olga. They are at the station to file a formal complaint against Victor, and my presence is demanded."

We hurry back to the station. Diego is sitting at a small computer table behind the counter while Olga and Valeria sit in chairs in the reception area. Valeria's hair covers her face as she hangs her head. Olga's gaze flicks about the room, her mouth tensely set. Not a hint of a smile. Army motions for the two of them to follow him into his office. I sit on a bench in reception and wait. Minutes later, they leave. Army comes out of his office looking pale and worn out. "I have a complaint number. I will ask Victor to voluntarily submit a DNA sample."

"Am I coming with you?" I ask.

"No, I will do this alone." He closes his eyes and puts his hands out in front of him, his lips set in a firm line. "I will be back. Please wait as Emilio and José Luis will be here soon."

I move to sit behind Army's desk. The minutes slowly tick by. After an hour, I can't help wondering how the conversation with Victor is going. In the meantime, I pull out an evidence folder containing the photos taken in the shed at the old sugar mill, hoping for inspiration, but none comes. Finally, Emilio saunters into the station with José right behind him. I tuck the pictures back in the envelope and place it facedown on the desk.

"Where is *he*?" Emilio jerks his head toward Army's office. "What is this new evidence? How long will this take?"

"On his way, don't know, and not sure," I blandly reply.

"Huh?" Emilio says.

"The answers to your questions."

He glares at me and mutters, "Estúpido," then drops into the wooden chair next to José, pulls out his phone, and starts texting. José Luis snickers and stares at the floor, but says nothing. I get up to pour myself a cup of coffee. I raise the cup and look at Emilio. He nods. I pour a cup and hand it to him. José declines. One set of familial DNA will be enough.

Army comes through the door a few minutes later. Emilio jumps up. "You have wasted my time. Can we get this over?"

Army smiles. "In a minute." He speaks quietly in Spanish to Diego, who nods, but doesn't move. Army then gestures for both Emilio and José to step into his office. I follow behind. Army walks to the chair behind the desk. I move a chair from in front of it to sit to Army's left. Emilio and José occupy chairs directly in front of the desk.

Army says, "I have asked you both here to clear up some questions as to Ana María's estate and who controls it."

"I do not understand," replies José. "I do."

Army shows José Luis the form authorizing Emilio to act on his behalf in liquidating Ana's estate. José raises his eyes and glares at Emilio. "I never signed this."

Emilio places his hand on José's shoulder and calmly replies, "Sí, mi hermano. You did. You were distraught at the loss of your wife. I asked if you wished me to handle things, and you agreed."

José slaps Emilio's hand away. "No, I did not sign this. You had no right!" he spits out.

"You had no idea what you were doing. You would have ruined everything. I have the brains to make this work. You drove around in a circle for your job. You married a rich woman. You never had to work for anything. Eres un estúpido," Emilio snaps.

Army slides the paper back toward himself. "José Luis, what would you like to do in this situation?"

"Arrest him. He is a liar and a cheat. I am sure my accounts will show he stole from me."

Emilio jumps up from his chair and slams his fist on the desk. "This proves nothing. You do not want to fight me. I will make you all sorry. I have made something of myself and have friends in high places."

"No, mi hermano. You have made me feel stupid my whole life. No more."

"You cannot prove you did not sign this. Why did you not die in that crash? I would have inherited everything."

A slow smile creases José's lips. "I will swear to it in court, but then there are the other papers from your business you asked me to keep at my house. I looked at them and know you forged signatures of people who could not read on contracts for you to steal their land." José looks directly at Army. "Would you be interested in those documents?"

Emilio jams his finger in José's face. "Do not! I knew you would never be anything. You can speak to my attorney, now. I did not hire that truck driver." He spins on his heels to leave.

I jump up and block his way. He stops and glares at me, but doesn't try to get past, as Army asks, "José, will you swear this is not your signature?"

José nods.

"One more thing." Army looks back at Emilio. "I have a forensic report linking the sugar cane fibers from your shed at the old mill with ones found on Juan Mercado's body." He pulls out his handcuffs. "Emilio, I am arresting you on suspicion of forgery, conspiracy to commit fraud, grand theft, and murder."

I must admit a certain feeling of satisfaction with seeing Emilio in handcuffs. Army speaks to Diego in Spanish, then turns to me. "Diego will take everything to Guadalajara. Emilio needs to be processed and jailed there, and his DNA swabs will go to the lab. You and I will accompany José Luis to his home to retrieve the documents he mentioned."

Army and Diego move Emilio to a squad car. Emilio mutters in Spanish in a tone that sounds guttural and threatening. His eyes reflect pure anger. Army's face is a blank mask.

Once Diego leaves, we turn our attention to José Luis. He smiles. "That is the first time in my life I have stood up to my brother." He sighs, and his shoulders visibly relax. "Come to my house, and I will give you the papers."

At his house, we follow him into an office, where he opens the top drawer of the desk. José sheepishly hands Army a stack of documents. "I am sorry for the hurt my brother caused. I did not kill my wife. I loved her."

Army nods. "A call was made from your phone the day of the crash to the truck driver that hit you. Can you explain that?"

José shakes his head. "No. That afternoon, Ana María and I had stopped at Emilio's house because he was settling her late father's estate and had papers for her to sign. I know I had my phone when the accident happened. I lost so much."

"Thank you for this." Army holds up the papers. "I am sorry it came at the cost of having your brother arrested."

"For the first time in a long time, I feel free of him. My silence cost many good people a lot. I should have been a better man."

Army and I shake José's hand farewell. We arrive home to find Karen and Eva in the murder room, discussing theories. Army and I watch and listen through the cracked-open door.

"Dos Hermanos means two brothers. Who do we know are brothers? Emilio and José Luis; Victor and Alejo," Karen says.

Eva breaks in, "I do not see Alejo being involved in dirty, smelly, difficult cattle rustling, do you?"

"No. He won't even help paint, the jerk." Karen giggles. "There is another set of brothers."

Eva cocks her head to one side. "Who?"

"Army and Juan," Karen replies. Eva bursts out laughing, and that's when I push the door open further and step into the room. "Hey, careful who you accuse."

Eva's eyes are dancing with delight as she looks at Army. "Mi amor, I would not ever believe that of you, but just to be sure, did you steal the cattle?"

Army crosses his arms across his chest. "Maybe . . ." We begin laughing like old friends do. "Any theories?" I ask.

Karen shakes her head. "I don't see Emilio or even José Luis getting their hands dirty. I guess they could have hired men to do the rustling and are the brains of the gang instead."

"Emilio and José do not like each other," Army jumps in. "I doubt they would be in business together."

I stare at the name Mateo Pérez on the board. "The truck driver that killed Ana María has the same last name as the manager at the Smith Cattle Processing Plant. Any way to check if *they're* brothers?"

Army's eyes light up. "The crime would be nearly perfect. One delivers the cows and the other makes them disappear. Let me make some calls." He pulls out his phone. After a few minutes and a lot of Spanish, Army beams. "They are brothers. I think we need to have another talk with Mr. Carlos Pérez.

CHAPTER 23

Army and I arrive back at the Smith Cattle Processing Plant and make our way to the office. As we walk through the door, both bodyguards jump to attention from the couch they were lounging on. Carlos Pérez looks up and snaps, "¿Ahora qué?"

I stand behind Army as he sits in a chair in front of Carlos' desk. "Please, speak English for my partner, please. We have a few follow-up questions. I understand your brother, Mateo, is a truck driver and has been charged with some serious crimes. What can you tell me about the cattle rustling ring?" Army leans back in his seat.

The color drains from Carlos' face. "I . . . I . . . I do not know what you mean."

"You were found in possession of stolen cattle. I want cooperation, or I will charge you with receiving stolen property and impeding an official police investigation. Was Mateo the driver of the truck that delivered the cows?"

"Mateo has nothing to do with this. I chose to not ask any questions when the cattle came in. I was given paperwork, and I processed it as valid. It is safer that way."

Army swipes through pictures on his phone, stopping at one. "Did you deal with this man?"

Carlos shakes his head. He's shown a second picture and acknowledges that one.

"Gracias." Army stands to leave, and I follow him to the truck.

Once in the driver's seat, Army drums his fingers on the steering wheel. "What's up?" I ask.

"He has identified my brother-in-law, Victor, as the man he dealt with." He sighs. "I need to secure a warrant to search Victor's home and any properties. I do not fully trust Carlos, but if it is true, it will kill Sara." His phone rings. "¡Bueno! . . . Sí . . . Sí . . . Gracias." He turns to me. "An arrest warrant arrived. Victor has been charged with first-degree sexual assault. I need to arrest him and have him processed."

"Am I going with you?"

"Not now. Thank you, but Diego and I will handle things. I need someone fluent in Spanish."

"Anything I can help with?" I empathize for my friend. This job is hard enough, but the hurt in the family is terrible.

"No, this I must do alone." Army puts the truck in gear. "I will drop you off at home."

"Drop me off at the hacienda. I'll check in with Karen and Eva. Are you adding cattle rustling charges?"

"I want to first execute the warrant and search his property. If I find any evidence he is involved, then they will be added."

The hacienda is busy with a crew of painters working on the exterior. I stop for a few minutes to take it all in before seeking out Karen, who's on the side of the building. "How's it goin'? It looks wonderful."

"It's great," she replies with a big smile. "Juan contacted his customers and asked for volunteers. A couple of professional painters showed up with a crew and supplies. We're almost done."

I follow her into the living room, where she hands me a brush and container of paint and asks me to do some touch-up work. While I paint, I can't help but think of how it's going with Army. So many lives disrupted, many close to home. What will be the extent of the damage done to Army's family and community? I force myself to focus on the project, which helps a couple of hours pass before Karen checks on me. "This is perfect. Thank you."

"Do you think tonight you and I can sit and look through the evidence at the house? I need your thoughts on everything, and Army has enough goin' on." Karen nods in agreement.

A few hours later, the both of us walk into the evidence room. I move Victor's name under the cattle rustlings case, and Emilio's is under the crash. Our focus is on the murders, the attempted murder, and the evidence to date. Pictures of the victims and the boot print, which is missing the right corner of the right heel and was at all the scenes, are on the wall. The forensic report linking fibers from the old sugar mill shed to the ones found on Juan Mercado's body is also there. I place a second card with Victor's name under the murder.

Karen stares at the wall. "Finding a match to the wire in the garrote will open the cases up."

I agree.

We hear footsteps approaching from the hall and look to see Army stick his head inside. "I arrested and processed Victor for the sexual assault warrant. DNA and arrest photos have been taken. He made bail already, but I have a search warrant for his house and property on the cattle rustling charges. I will go tonight."

"I don't know if I should say 'Good luck' or not."

Army shrugs. "I heard you and Karen discussing the wire. I will be sure the team collects all they find."

"Checking boots, too?" I ask.

"¡Sí! Buenas noches," Army says as he waves goodbye. A few minutes later, we hear the Trailblazer pull out of the driveway. Part of me wants to be there, but the other part of me knows that this is not my investigation. I find that I'm restless. I try to read and watch TV, but end up pacing instead. Karen and Eva are at the kitchen table, making a list of things that need to be finished at the hacienda. I'm a little lost, not being a part of that either.

Then it dawns on me. I can be part of the investigation, at least covertly.

"I'm taking a walk," I announce.

Karen and Eva simultaneously look up at me. Karen knits her eyebrows together. "Would you like us to come with?"

"Nooo . . . umm, no," I mumble.

Karen looks at me suspiciously but doesn't say anything more. I hurry to the garage and check Army's workbench, grab a pair of wire cutters, and quickly head for Marcyellene's house. She had previously mentioned that Victor installed electric fencing in her yard to keep out Ernesto, with no success. If the wire is still there, I plan to secure a piece for comparison. I'm wearing dark clothes and walk casually as if out for an evening stroll.

I pass no one, and the streets are devoid of cars. In my mind, I roll over and over the consequences for Victor if the wires match. I understand I will bring more pain to this family. Wait, someone tried to kill my friend, and did kill two others, so forget the consequences. Of course, if Marcyellene is involved, that may just be a bonus.

I arrive at the house. It's dark. Good. She must be busy with *another* committee meeting. Whatever the reason, dark is good.

I walk the perimeter of her yard, wait for my eyes to adjust, and grope for the downed wire.

"BLEAT." I spin on my heels. Ernesto is inches away from me. *"BLEAT."*

"Shhh." I realize I just shushed a goat. His reply is a blank stare as he chews more of Marcyellene's flowers. After several minutes of searching, I'm able to locate the wire and cut a fair length. With both the wire and cutter secured in my pocket, I move to the sidewalk. Ernesto follows me, but turns in the opposite direction, leaving a trail of goat pellets the entire length of Marcyellene's house. I snicker at his irreverence and secretly applaud his attitude toward someone who wishes him dead. An air of satisfaction comes over me for my mission.

Once home, I notice that Karen and Eva have gone to bed. I check the piece against the picture and realize that the fencing wire is much thicker. Deflated, I drop the wire and cutters on the counter. I plan to wait up for Army, so I turn on the TV and surf for an English-speaking channel.

I wake up on the couch as early morning light fills the room and smell the comforting scent of coffee. Looking toward the kitchen, Army is sitting at the table. After a quick stretch, I grab a cup and join him. "Okay, details."

Army laughs. "Well, we collected several bags of evidence, including wire of all kinds, but none matched the one we have in evidence. I brought home the actual wire from the scene of my attack. I do not know whether to be happy or not. At this point, I cannot prove Victor is a murderer."

"Anything else?"

"I have guards posted at the sites so nothing is tampered with. There are several remote buildings on his property we did not get to search. We will go back today. Would you like to come?"

"I thought you'd never ask." We clink coffee mugs. I give him a recap of my mission from the previous night. He is out loud laughing when Eva and Karen join us. Eva rubs Army's shoulders, and he pats her hands and nods. Events are shared and plans made. Karen kisses the top of my head. "Be safe . . . please?"

"You know me. I'm a cockroach. Little gets to me." I wink.

"Eva and I are doing a walk through the hacienda," she states. "We'll refine our last-minute to-do list. Sara is staying home, given what's happening. So, I'll be busy today."

I nod, but find it hard to contain the excitement of being in on the investigation again.

Eva and Karen head out, and Army and I drive to Victor's property. Army gives a wave to Diego, who's standing guard at the end of the driveway. We drive in the direction of a large, wooden, shotgun-style shed. In front of the door, Jesús is waving his arms wildly. Army throws the truck in 'park,' jumps out, and walks to him. Jesús makes slashing marks, looks to the heavens, and points to the door, all while rapidly speaking Spanish. Ernesto is slowly munching his way into the field.

Army listens to Jesús, nods, and replies. Jesús removes a small bottle from his jacket, pulls off the top, and throws a clear liquid on the shed door. The bottle empty, he wanders after Ernesto.

Army tightly presses his lips together before speaking. "Jesús is convinced those are claw marks of the Chupacabra on the door. He blessed the shed with holy water and feels it is now safe for us to enter." Army stares at me as if expecting a response.

"I got nothing," I reply.

"Good," Army states and pulls back the shed door. He stops in his tracks, and I run right into him. I see the reason. Before us is large cattle-hauling semi-trailer. I step around him and check the tires. One has the distinctive gash that was present at the known rustling. This confirms Victor's involvement.

Army sighs. "We will need to process it for prints and other evidence." We know the drill. We head to the rear of the Trailblazer. I grab the fingerprint kit, and Army grabs the camera. We each focus on our tasks. First, Army photographs the entire scene, then bags and tags samples from each of the semi's tires. I dust and lift prints off the most touchable surfaces outside the semi, then open the truck's passenger side door and dust the interior of the cab before reaching inside the glove box. I place various items in evidence bags, such as a package of gum, napkins, and plastic utensils. Also inside is a spiral-bound notebook. "Hey, look at this."

Army walks over and sees what I'm holding. "Do not tell me the thieves kept a record of their crimes?"

"Not sure. It's written in Spanish," I say, handing the book to him.

He flips through the pages. "It has names and locations of area farmers. I think this is a formula, to not duplicate thefts. There are maps, herd sizes, a calendar, even a record of cash payments to men involved in each incident. Unfortunately, only initials were used to identify them. Victor even has his herd in here, but I'm sure it was to not create suspicion of why his was the only local cattle not stolen. This was well-organized. I'll spend some time going through the book to see if I can put names to those initials."

After the truck and trailer, the only other item in the shed is a cabinet in the corner. "Can you photograph this?" I ask. "I'll dust for prints, then we can open it."

When we're finished, Army breaks the lock. Inside are Bluetooth-capable, two-way radios, headsets, and additional batteries. We process all the equipment. The evidence packaged and secured, we head to the station. I copy the logbook while Army marks everything into evidence. Diego transports all of it to the crime lab in Guadalajara for DNA and additional testing. We're close to solving the cattle rustling crimes and hopefully the murders will be right behind, but who will be exposed? A mixture of anticipation and anxiety race through my mind as I review our list of suspects.

"Come, amigo, let's get something to eat. I will buy lunch at the Hotel del Sol," Army announces.

"You're speaking my language."

It's only a short walk to the hotel. We enter the restaurant and find a table near the back with a clear view of the door. I smile. Cop habits never die. The only other people here are a group of six men, who motion for the waitress, pay, and quickly make their way to the door. Army has his elbows on the table, his fingertips pressed together, and his eyes laser-focused on the men who just left.

"Okay . . . who are they?" I ask.

"Well, that's interesting. I saw the initials A.G. in the logbook. I thought it was for Alejo Guerrero, but one of those men was Antonio Guerrero, Victor's youngest brother. Last I heard, he was at the university in México City. So, what is he doing here?"

"And the others with him?"

"Men we saw at the old stockyard when we first investigated the cattle rustling."

"That's right. One of them was the guy that called me away from the pens when I found the tire track."

A busboy is making his way to the abandoned table when Army jumps up and heads over. He secures the glasses and cutlery. "Dan, grab paper and chart this table for me." Army points to the chairs and provides names for each man sitting there. He asks me to watch over the table while he returns to the station for the evidence kit. Once he's back, we process each piece for fingerprints and swab for DNA, then bag and tag the items. Army smiles. "I think Diego will be making a second trip to the lab today. I'm sure some of these prints will match those found in the semi and on the radios in Victor's shed, as well as some of the initials.

"What about lunch?" I ask. Army laughs. "Let's order. I will secure these items at the station, call Diego, and be back before lunch is served."

Food ordered and evidence secured, we sit down to a nice lunch and a few rounds of tequila, talking and completely relaxed.

CHAPTER 24

Karen is up early the next morning. "The grand opening of the hacienda is in a few days, and there are a bunch of little things that still need to be done."

"Anything I can help with?" I ask.

She shakes her head. "No, Eva is picking up a few more accessories at the market, and I'm gonna head over and do some staging. We can meet there this afternoon."

"Okay, Army and I'll stop by later. If you need help moving anything, let us know."

Karen leans in and kisses me. "Thanks. I'm so excited to see this pulled together."

"I'm glad for you. It seems as if Army and I are close to solving several cases. I promise that then we'll have a real vacation," I say, wiggling my eyebrows at her.

"Ugh," she replies as she playfully slaps my chest.

Army and I drive to Victor's house. We're standing on the porch as my eyes glance to the immaculate flower beds. *Karen would know the names of all these plants.* They appear well-tended and hydrated, even with the water shortage. As I glance over them, I notice a boot print in the recently watered dirt. The right heel is missing the right corner. I'm about to get

Army's attention when Victor opens the door. If he knows why we're there, his face doesn't reveal it.

"¡Buenos días! ¿Cómo estás?" he says sarcastically. He positions himself in the doorframe.

Army easily pushes past him into the foyer. "Do you know why we are here, Victor?"

"I do not. Are you here as Comisario General or as my brother-in-law?"

Arrogant jerk.

"This is professional," Army calmly replies. "We suspect you of being the head of the cattle rustling ring."

A sly smile crosses Victor's face. "Suspect, but cannot prove?"

Army smiles back. "Let me rephrase that. You *are* the head, and I can prove it."

"How?" Victor asks, his eyes widening.

"Dan and I went to the local slaughterhouse. There was a cow there with blood on her horn. Not just any blood, but *human* blood. Your blood. DNA confirms it. How do you explain that?"

Victor waves his hand in a dismissive manner. "Any number of ways. As a cattle rancher, I'm always looking at cattle. It would not be the first time one of them drew my blood."

Army shakes his head. "I am sure that is true, but this is not one of your cows. It belongs to a Señor Tomás Blanco, and he said that cow along with others were stolen from his place."

Victor's arrogant smile returns. "I have done business with him many times over the years. In fact, I was just at his place four or five days ago. I remember a cow stabbing me with her horn that day."

I want to slap that smile off his face. But Army's good at what he does.

"The problem is that two nights ago there was a terrible rainstorm," he says. "His cows were in an open field. No protection of any kind. He checked on them the next day, and all of them were soaked. His cattle were stolen that night. We found them at the slaughterhouse the next morning. It is not possible that fresh blood would be on the horns. So, you must have been there at the time the cattle were stolen, and you were injured at that time. There's also a wealth of evidence we found in your shed. Stop acting as if I am stupid. I am placing you under arrest for cattle rustling. Turn around and place your hands behind your back."

Victor stands defiant and glares at Army, whose face is expressionless. Army turns Victor around by the shoulders, and Victor yields as he's cuffed. We step out onto the porch.

I look down, point, and ask, "Who's boot print is in your flower bed?"

Victor sneers with an incredulous look. "Who cares about flower beds? Estúpido gringo."

Army peeks over the porch to look at what I'm pointing to. He spins Victor around to face him. "Just answer the man's question. Who does that boot print belong to?"

"My idiot brother. Ever since leaving college, which I paid for, he has no real job, but he has time to weed my flowers."

"Antonio?" Army asks.

"What? No, the other idiot, Alejo," Victor spits.

"Army, I've got a bad feeling about this. We gotta go," I say.

Army hurries Victor off the porch toward the Trailblazer. "What? Where? Why?"

"I think Alejo is our killer, and Karen is alone at the hacienda. I just need to be sure she is all right. Where is Alejo right now?" I demand.

Victor spats, "I do not know."

If he's telling the truth or not, we need to get to the hacienda, soon.

Victor hits his head on the doorframe as Army shoves him into the back seat. "Watch your head." Victor shoots him a nasty look. Army and I jump in the front, and he drops the car in gear, hits the gas, and peels out onto the street.

Outside the hacienda, I'm out of the truck before it completely stops. "Karen, Karen." I run through the courtyard. "*KAREN.*"

"Here. I'm in the living room," she replies.

I charge into the room to find Karen holding a sword on Alejo. He's lying on the ground, dressed like a conquistador. A garrote lies next to him.

"Are you all right?" I ask. Karen hands me the sword.

"No, she hit me with a chair," Alejo whines.

Scoffing, I reply, "Shut up. I'm not talking to *you.*"

A nervous laugh escapes from Karen. "I was moving a mirror when I noticed the wire Alejo had used to hang it. It looked like the piece found at the scene of Army's attack. That's when I caught his reflection and saw him coming up behind me."

Army pulls Alejo up by his arm and cuffs him.

I am in total awe of my wife. "How did you get away?"

"Before he could get that thing around my neck, I dropped to the floor and rolled sideways. I was scrambling to find a weapon to hit him with when Ernesto came running out of nowhere and rammed him from behind. I jumped up, grabbed a chair, and hit him, then I picked up his sword to hold him. I was reaching for my phone when I heard you yell and knew I'd be okay," Karen replies triumphantly.

"Alejo Guerrero, you are under arrest for several murders, a few attempted murders, and *bad* fashion sense." Army grunts a laugh.

"Why are you dressed like a conquistador?" I ask.

Alejo's eyes glaze over, and he starts speaking in rapid Spanish that I don't understand.

Army shakes his head. "Apparently, Spain will rise again to be a world power over us peasants, crushing our uncivilized population. I am thinking he may have grounds for an insanity defense." Army leads Alejo away, who is still muttering.

I grab Karen in a hug, and I'm not sure I'll never let her go again. This could have ended very badly.

She snorts a laugh. "I think I captured another murderer."

Kissing the top of her head, I reply, "Yes. Yes, you have. The other detective in the family. Let's go back to the house."

The next morning, Army joins Karen, Eva, and I at the kitchen table. He got in after we all went to bed, so he's working on only a few hours of sleep.

"Alejo has completely lost it," he says. "He continues to rant about the rise of Spain over us heathens. However, during one lucid moment, he talked about everything that happened."

"What did he say?" I ask.

"Juan Mercado saw him paying off the truck driver that killed Ana María and was supposed to kill José Luis. He was at Emilio's house that day and used José's cell phone to set up the crash. Mr. Mercado said he would arrange for Perros Bastardos to buy Alejo's land for the water park and asked for a percentage of the money. Alejo was afraid his 'empire' was in jeopardy, so he decided to eliminate Mr. Mercado and deal directly with the owner of the company."

"How did he get Juan Mercado to Emilio's outbuilding at the old sugar mill?" Karen inquires.

Army snorts a laugh. "He called as Emilio, promising another payoff if the company would agree to buy Emilio's land. Apparently, Emilio was working his own deal with Juan Mercado. Alejo waited for him to show up. He killed him there but moved the body to appear as if Emilio were framing him. He knew we would figure out that Mr. Mercado was not killed where we found him."

I sigh. "It almost worked. Why kill Brad?"

"Alejo was inside the hacienda in the conquistador outfit when Brad showed up unexpectedly. He panicked and killed him, but then realized he might scare off the Preservation Committee from finishing the place. He was going to buy it for little or nothing and make it his 'Spanish Jewel.' His words."

"Why did he use a garrote?" I ask.

Karen jumps in, "Because it's a silent way to kill."

Army shakes his head. "He corrected me on that. It is *not* a garrote, but rather a *Spanish windlass.* Apparently, anything to do with Spain is good."

"What about the other stuff?" Eva asks. "The attack on you, then pictures and threats, and why the Chupacabra claw?"

"Everything was designed to scare people and divert suspicion away from him and Victor."

"His brother was involved?" I say.

"Not in the murder. Alejo knew Victor was the head of the cattle rustling ring and was photographing him in case he needed to blackmail Victor later. Dos Hermanos is run by Victor and Antonio Guerrero, two brothers. Alejo saw me on the stakeout and was concerned I would ruin his plan, so he attacked. He also sent the pictures hoping it would stop the investigation. Guerrero means warrior, so the Conquistador Company was born."

"The blank business card with the conquistador helmet was Victor's," Karen says. "So, the warning at the ruins, 'Beware the warrior. Maintain your guard always,' meant all the brothers, and again at the hacienda when Señora María said, 'The conquistador brings evil.' I didn't put it all together until just now. Was Marcyellene involved in any of these crimes?"

Army shakes his head. "No, she is just self-involved and self-serving. Her only interests are in anything and anyone that could benefit her. She was having an affair with Victor, who is not the father of Valeria's baby. DNA eliminated him and has not indicated anyone in our system. I am not sure who is. Valeria's aunt did call me and said that Valeria has been in love with José since she was a child. Valeria's father kicked her out of the house, and she was desperate to find a way to support herself and her baby. She had slept with José, once, and hoped he would not question the parenthood of the baby, but would marry her and give the baby a name and her a standing in the community. She also slept with Victor, but it was not assault. At least, that is what she is saying now."

Karen touches Army's arm. "How is Sara doing?"

Army shrugs. "She is very sad and embarrassed at Víctor's crime. The family will be there for her and make sure she and the kids are all right. We will try and keep the legitimate cattle business going too."

"I'm sorry, my friend. This is a lot to deal with," I say.

"It is, but as family we will get through it. I am happy that we have the answers we needed. People in town can relax," Army says. "Speaking of relaxing, you and Karen deserve a vacation. It starts now. Eva and I want to hear some of the things you would like to do here in México."

"After the opening of the hacienda, mi amor," Eva chimes in.

"I want to see all our hard work to the end. We can make it a great party, and you know how I love to plan a party," Karen replies with a giant grin.

"And a *HUGE* thank-you gift goes to Ernesto," I add. Everyone nods in agreement.

The next morning, we all head to the hacienda. Marco has delivered the last of the furniture and accessories, so we finish staging the entire house. Preservation Committee members show up with food. The mariachi band sets up and begins playing, the balloons are out, punch has been made, and we open the gates to the courtyard. The turnout is fabulous. We spend hours smiling, talking, and answering questions, surrounded by positive energy and music. All the visitors approve. A few try to pump Army on information about the resolution of the crimes, but he laughs and waves them off.

I'm standing in the living room when Karen enters with tears in her eyes. "What's wrong?" I ask.

"Nothing. I was speaking with Señora María. She said that the place is more beautiful than she remembers."

"Right. She was here when you first started the project and had definite opinions on what needed to happen," I reply.

"Her comment made all the work worth it. I'd like to introduce you." We step out into the courtyard. Karen scans the crowd. "That's her. The elderly lady, wearing the black lace dress, sitting on the fountain wall."

I don't see anyone sitting there. I look at Karen, who turns to me, then back, and points. "She's right there, Dan." Still no one there. Karen looks back at fountain. "Where could she have gone? She was there a minute ago."

I hug her. "It doesn't matter. Everything is beautiful, and you're a big reason for it."

I know Karen has a list of sites for us to visit in Mexico. I am ready for a vacation with her and these good friends.